A SEAGROVE CHRISTMAS

RACHEL HANNA

CHAPTER ONE

*T*here was just something about Christmas.

It had always been Julie's favorite holiday, and having a new son had only made it more special this year. Even though she had Vivi too, a son was different than a granddaughter.

She could watch her new son grow into a man every day. She fed him, cleaned up his skinned knees, and made him do his homework. Being a grandmother was a part-time job, and it was usually only the fun stuff. Being a mom meant doing the hard stuff, too.

She watched as Dawson held Dylan on his shoulders next to the Christmas tree. They had to get an artificial one because Dylan was allergic to the real ones, and she had to admit she kind of liked the big fake one. It was perfectly symmetrical and didn't drop needles all over her floor. Plus, it had given her an excuse to go out and buy a bunch of Christmas ornaments to inaugurate the new tree.

This year, she'd gone with a blue and silver theme.

Dawson said it reminded him of a Christmas tree Elvis might've had at Graceland, but Julie didn't let it bother her. She was full of joy this holiday season, and none of her husband's teasing was going to get her riled up.

"Reach higher," Dawson said, rising up on his tiptoes so that Dylan could put the flashy silver star on the top.

"Don't you boys knock my tree over, or I'll throw those freshly baked chocolate chip cookies right into the ocean out there!"

Dylan giggled. She loved the sound of his laughter. After seeing him those first few times at the camp, she'd wondered what it would take to see him happy again. He'd gone through so much in his brief life, with his mother's abandonment and the death of his father. All she wanted now was for him to live a long, healthy, happy life, and she would do whatever she had to to make that happen.

"Got it!" Dylan said, out of breath from reaching as far as his little arms would take him. Dawson lowered him to the ground, and Dylan dramatically fell back onto the floor, splayed out like he'd just run a marathon.

"Now, go grab that box of ornaments from the attic," Dawson directed. He was firm with his new son, which was a different side of Dawson she hadn't seen before. He wanted to grow him into a good, solid man and upstanding citizen. He was the kindest father Julie had ever seen. Sometimes, she found herself wishing she'd raised her children with him instead of Michael, but then she wouldn't have had Colleen and Meg. Regrets were useless anyway.

"Do you think he can carry that big box down the

stairs?" Julie asked as she craned her head, watching him run up the stairs.

Dawson chuckled. "I wouldn't have sent him otherwise. Besides, I needed a minute alone with my hot wife." He grabbed her hand and pulled her close, pressing his lips to hers. That just never got old.

"Yeah, we don't get a lot of alone time anymore, do we?" she said, smiling.

"No, but it's so worth it. I know he's eight years old, but I feel like he's always been my son." Her heart swelled when he said things like that. Dawson gave Dylan all the attention a father should give, and she knew what a blessing that was for both of them.

"He's almost nine, you know," she said. It was the day after Thanksgiving, and Dylan would turn nine on Sunday. They had a big family dinner planned, and she couldn't wait to see the look on his face when he got the video gaming system he'd wanted so badly. Dawson had already said he was going to impose limits on it. He didn't want his son to stare at a screen all day. The environment outside was way too rich and beautiful to ignore and stare at a fake world.

Julie heard Dylan bounding back down the stairs, breaking their intimate moment. "This thing is heavy!"

"Use those muscles, boy!" Dawson said as he walked over and met him at the bottom of the stairs. He took the box from Dylan.

"Can I go get a snack from Miss Lucy?"

"Miss Lucy is with her family this week, remember?" Julie said, reminding him. Lucy loved cooking for Dylan. She often said he reminded her of her grandson. Dawson had given her the week off to go spend time with him and the rest of her family in Mississippi, so they'd had to fend for themselves on Thanksgiving.

Dawson had done an outstanding job with the turkey, while Dixie had brought the most delicious stuffing. Janine, the world's worst cook, had smartly brought a pre-made cake from a bakery. SuAnn brought pound-cake, of course, and Julie had cooked the sides. It had been the most fun Thanksgiving she'd ever had. Every person she loved was sitting around the table, and that was more than she could ever ask for in her life.

"I forgot," Dylan said.

"But there are some snacks in the fridge. Just don't eat too much before bed, okay?"

"Yes, ma'am," he said before he scurried off into the kitchen.

Dawson opened the box and looked at Julie. "How are we supposed to get more ornaments on this tree?"

"We aren't putting them all on there. This box has some family ornaments that I'd like to put up, though. Like this one," she said, pulling one out of the tissue paper and smiling. "Colleen made this in third grade."

"Aw. A cute little doggie," Dawson said, taking it from her hand.

Julie stared at him. "It's a snowman."

Dawson laughed. "Glad she didn't become an artist." She smacked him on the arm playfully.

"And look at this. My grandmother knitted this little stocking ornament when Meg was born."

He smiled. "You know what I love about this Christmas?"

"What?"

"That it's now our family. Not yours and not mine. Ours."

She smiled and kissed him on the cheek. "Forever."

* * *

Colleen stared at the computer screen, trying to get her eyes to focus. Thanksgiving had been so much fun, but she'd eaten too much, couldn't sleep, and she was still exhausted. Besides, who wanted to work at all during the holiday season?

"How's it coming?" Tucker asked, walking up behind her. Everyone else in the office was off today, but they had work to do if his new toy was going to take off this holiday season.

"Well, I just sent the report to Ted, and the numbers are looking great. You know we're on the best toy list for this Christmas season?"

Tucker grinned. "Seriously? Oh, Colleen, I think this might be our big break!"

She stood up and faced him. "I'm so proud of you, Tuck. All the hard work is paying off."

He pulled her into a tight embrace. "I couldn't do any of this without my best friend. Thanks for believing in me, Colleen."

"Always."

As they stood there, hugging in her cubicle, she was so thankful to have found a man like Tucker. Some days, she didn't know what she did to deserve him. He was always kind to her and everyone else. He went out of his way to help people. He loved his career, and he was a kid at heart. Being around Tucker was pure joy.

"What do you say we go get some lunch?"

Colleen rubbed her stomach. "Great idea. I'm starving." She picked up her purse just as the phone on her desk rang. Sighing, she reached over and picked it up. "This is Colleen. How can I help you?" She listened for a moment, and then her mouth dropped open. "Can you hold just a moment, please?"

"What's wrong?"

"Tucker, that's Jamison O'Malley."

"What?"

"He wants to set up a meeting with you."

"Jamison O'Malley wants to meet with me? About what?" The CEO of the largest toy manufacturer was hanging on the line to talk to her boyfriend, and Colleen felt like she couldn't breathe. This was like the President of the United States calling.

"I don't know, sweetie. But I don't think keeping him on hold is the best idea."

Tucker nodded quickly and took the phone. As he answered, his voice vibrating slightly at the beginning, Colleen felt her heartbeat quicken. This was a big deal, and she knew it. Tucker deserved all the good things, and she was certain this was the start of something big.

* * *

Hen pinched off a piece of the cinnamon apple pound-cake that SuAnn had given her and stuffed it into her mouth like she hadn't eaten in days. "I swear I've gained ten pounds since we stopped hating each other."

SuAnn rolled her eyes. "Would you rather we went back to hating each other then?"

Hen thought for a moment. "No. I'm too addicted now." She wiped her mouth and took a sip of her sweet tea, the rush of sugar surely flying through her veins.

"So, I actually came today because I have some news for you."

"What kind of news?" SuAnn asked, biting into her piece of pound-cake and realizing that it needed more cinnamon. She made a mental note and then went back to listening to Hen prattle on about whatever it was she was talking about.

"Are you listening to me?"

"What? Yes. I'm just thinking about a recipe."

Hen rolled her eyes. "I said that the Seagrove Christmas Festival is coming up in a couple of weeks, and my husband wants you to have a big table there. There's also going to be a cakewalk game, and we want you to provide some cakes. What do you say?"

Hen's husband was the mayor, and she had grown to like him pretty well, although she didn't see him nearly as much as she saw Hen.

"Of course. Just give me the details, and I'll bake whatever we need."

Hen finished her cake and stood up. "Well, I'd better get out of here. I have a meeting at the botanical gardens, and then my book club meets tonight. Are you sure you don't want to join? It's a hoot!"

SuAnn rolled her eyes and laughed. "Hang out with a bunch of old biddies and talk about books? No, thank you."

Hen waved her hand at SuAnn as she walked toward the door. "You're so silly! I'll see you later, you irritable old bird!"

As SuAnn watched Hen walk down the sidewalk and around the corner, she couldn't help but be thankful for their new friendship. It seemed like no one really "got her", but Hen did. They were two of a kind, and she wasn't always sure that was a good thing.

"Sorry I'm late!" Darcy said as she breezed in through the back door of the bakery. Her hair was flying all over the place, her purse falling off her shoulder. "My son was sick all night, and then my sitter was late showing up. I got no sleep, but here I am!"

"Well, you look dreadful, dear. Maybe you should go clean yourself up a bit in the bathroom? Don't want to scare the customers."

Darcy glared at her. "Wow, thanks, SuAnn. You know how to make a girl feel good about herself." She put her purse under the cash register and turned toward the bathroom.

"Honesty is the best policy!" SuAnn called to her as Darcy slammed the door.

* * *

Dixie scurried around her house, trying to get everything as clean as possible. She felt like the Queen was coming, but it was only Harry's daughter, Carrie. Although she'd been married to Harry for months, she had yet to meet his one and only child. Carrie traveled a lot for her work, and she hadn't come to see her father since Dixie had met him. Although he spoke with her on the phone quite often, Dixie had never formally met her.

Harry had only told her that Carrie had been married at one time, to a doctor, and they'd divorced within three years of getting married. She'd been single for over a decade, with no kids, and was very focused on her career as an advertising executive. Most recently, she'd lived in Los Angeles and worked on some of the most famous advertising campaigns.

"What are you doing, woman?" Harry asked, shocked to see Dixie standing on a step stool, trying to clean the ceiling fan blades in the kitchen. He walked over and put his hand on her leg. "You're going to fall!"

"Oh, I certainly am not! I'm not an invalid, darlin'," she said, laughing. Of course, she wasn't about to admit that she'd almost fallen twice already.

"Get down from there," he said, picking her up around her legs and lowering her to the floor.

She smacked him playfully on the arm. Harry might've had Parkinson's disease, just like she did, but he was still as strong as an ox. Physical therapy had helped him maintain his muscles so far. That was a good thing because she needed him to be strong so they could keep traveling in their motorhome.

"Harry, your daughter will be here in a few minutes, and this place needs to look nice!"

He put his hands on her cheeks. "Listen to me, Dixie. Carrie isn't going to notice our ceiling fan blades or the dust bunny in the corner of the guest bathroom."

Dixie's mouth dropped open. "There's a dust bunny in there? Oh, Lord!" She moved past him quickly, picking up the broom that was leaning against the refrigerator on her way to the bathroom off the foyer.

"Honey, I think you're getting a little..."

Dixie's head swung around. "A little what?"

He cleared his throat. "Well, now, don't get your feathers ruffled when I say this, but you're acting a little... nutty..."

"Nutty?" She squinted her eyes at him. "Harry, don't

you go getting on my bad side today." She scooped up the dust bunny, tossed it into the trashcan and breezed past him to go back into the kitchen. Harry followed along like the devoted husband he was.

"Why are you getting so worked up over this, Dixie?"

She finally stopped and let out the big breath she'd been holding since she heard Carrie was coming to town. "Because she's your daughter. And my new step-daughter. I want her to like me."

Harry poked out his lip and put his hands on her shoulders. "Darlin', never in the history of this planet has there been a person who didn't like you."

She chuckled. "That ain't even a little bit true."

"Well, I sure can't imagine it. And my daughter is going to love you. The real you. Not this worked up, crazy, dust bunny hunting version of you. Just be yourself."

Dixie took in a deep breath and then blew it out. She knew he was right. There was no reason his daughter would hate her. She was just being dramatic again, something she did all too often. Everything would be fine.

Just as she was getting herself calmed down, there was a knock at the front door. She looked at her watch and knew it had to be Carrie, and her heart started racing all over again.

"Why don't we answer it together?" Harry said, putting his hand on her lower back. She nodded and walked toward the door.

It's funny, the weird things a person thinks to them-selves in stressful situations. For some reason, all she could think about right now was what outfit she'd chosen to wear. Her favorite pair of white jeans, a colorful Christmas sweater with a red bird on the front and a pair of sparkly white tennis shoes she'd bedazzled years ago with her bridge club. Maybe it was too much, but it was a little late to think about that now.

Harry opened the door, a huge smile on his face. "There's my beautiful daughter!" She stepped through the threshold and hugged her father tightly, not noticing Dixie yet.

"Daddy! I'm so glad to see your face in person! You look good!"

"Well, I feel as good as I did twenty years ago!" His deep voice bounced around the small foyer and caused Dixie to turn down her hearing aid a bit.

"You have Parkinson's," she said, laughing at what she thought was the absurdity of her father feeling good with a progressive disease.

"Honey, this thing doesn't control me. And I also have an amazing wife to share my life with, so it doesn't get much better!" He stepped back a bit and put his arm around Dixie like he was showing off his most prized possession. "Carrie, I'd like to introduce you to my wife, Dixie."

Dixie smiled nervously. She didn't get rattled easily, but she felt like she was meeting royalty or her favorite TV cooking show host.

"It's so nice to meet you, Carrie. Harry has bragged on you so much that I feel like I already know you."

Carrie, who looked like she just stepped out of a fashion magazine with her perfectly coiffed blond hair and her smooth, flawless skin, smiled. But it wasn't a genuine smile. It was the smile of someone who was trying to play a part. A woman could tell when another woman was faking a reaction, and she was certainly doing that. The question was, why?

"Nice to meet you, Dixie. Dad has spoken highly of you." She reached out her manicured hand, complete with French tipped nails, and shook Dixie's. Now, Dixie had grown up in the south, where girls were taught how to have a firm handshake. Carrie's handshake felt a bit like a dead fish, and she worried she might break the poor girl's delicate bones.

Harry pulled Dixie close to him and kissed the top of her head. "She's the best thing that's happened to me in years. You know, we'll start traveling again after Christmas, and we've got some big adventures planned!"

Carrie blew a quick breath out of her nose, almost imperceptibly, but Dixie noticed it, nonetheless. This girl had a problem with her, and she didn't know what it was. Happy holidays, Dixie thought to herself.

CHAPTER TWO

*D*arcy rang up the last customer of the day and walked out from behind the counter to lock the front door. It had been an exhausting day and she was ready to get home, eat dinner and crash into her bed. Having a small child, she knew the likelihood of going to bed early was slim to none.

Hatcher had recently started having nightmares, so she was waking up multiple times at night. Her husband, with his crazy work schedule, did his best to help, but he was often out of town, leaving Darcy to do most of the work with their son.

She locked the front door and turned to head back to the register, eager to balance it and get out of there. Covered in flour and smelling like straight sugar, she needed a hot bath and a nice cup of gingerbread hot tea to end her long day. Just as she was tallying up the day's profits, she heard someone tap on the glass door. It wasn't quite dark yet, but she couldn't quite see who was there until she walked closer.

An older gentleman, wearing a hat and a long coat, was standing there. He looked like something out of a movie, maybe a private investigator or sleuth. He had a white beard, reminding her a bit of Santa Claus, especially at this time of the year. She leaned a little to make sure he wasn't hiding a large bag of toys behind him.

Feeling a little worried that this random stranger was knocking on the door, she got as close as possible and spoke loudly. "Sorry, we're closed."

He smiled, which was a good sign that maybe he wasn't there to kill her. "I know, and I'm sorry to bother. I'm looking for SuAnn."

Maybe he was a private investigator. If anyone would have one chasing them, it would be SuAnn. There was no telling what that woman had done in her past.

"She's gone for the day," Darcy called back. He looked dejected by the idea that she wasn't there, and against Darcy's better judgment, she unlocked the door and opened it. "She left a few hours ago."

"Oh, darn! I'd hoped to see her. Will she be in tomorrow?"

Darcy chuckled. "Honestly, I never know. She's a bit... unpredictable."

Again, he smiled. "That sounds familiar."

"What was that?"

"Oh, nothing. I guess I'll check back tomorrow and see if she's around." He started to walk away.

"Hey, wait! What's your name?"

The man turned and smiled again. "Just tell her Nick stopped by."

Nick? She watched him walk down the street and around the corner, and she had to wonder who this

mysterious stranger was and what did he want with
SuAnn?

    * * *

SuAnn stared at her. "I don't know anyone named
Nick." She continued kneading the dough to make her
cinnamon apple bread.

"Well, he knows you, and he's coming back today to
see you."

"That's creepy."

"He looked a lot like Santa Claus, actually," Darcy
said, wiping down one of the tables.

SuAnn stopped and looked at her. "So, a guy named
Nick came looking for me, and he looks like Santa? Are
you sure someone wasn't playing a joke?"

"I don't think so. He seemed pretty serious about
it." Darcy walked over and turned the sign from closed
to open.

"Well, if Santa is coming to kidnap me, I guess there
are worse things," SuAnn said, rolling her eyes.

Darcy walked around the counter and picked up her
purse. "Okay, I'll be back in a couple of hours."

"Wait. Where are you going?"

Darcy sighed and shook her head. "You need to get
your memory checked. I have a dentist appointment
this morning, remember?"

"Oh, that's right," SuAnn said. She wasn't worried
about her memory. It wasn't that she couldn't remember
things; it was that she often wasn't interested in what
people were talking about. A bad personality trait, yes.
A memory problem, no. "Are you getting them
whitened?"

Darcy glared at her. "No, SuAnn. I'm getting a cavity

filled. Working at this place is going to make my teeth fall out from all the sugar." She walked toward the door.

"Still, a good whitening wouldn't be a waste of time!" SuAnn called behind her. She wasn't sure, but Darcy may have made a crude hand gesture at her through the plate-glass window.

"I was just trying to help," she muttered to herself. As she turned to pick up her ball of dough, her hip hit the counter and knocked an entire bowl of flour all over the floor. "Oh, good Lord!"

SuAnn hurriedly walked to the back room to get the broom and dustpan. She hated a mess, and since she was the only one working, she needed to get it cleaned up quickly. As soon as she crouched down to clean up, the bell on the door dinged to let her know a customer had come in.

The thing she loved about Hotcakes was that she had regular customers who came in every morning like clockwork. Mr. Dearen came for the hazelnut coffee. Esther with the ugly red cane came to get a bear claw even though she needed a salad more than a sweet treat. There were several people who always came in, and she knew exactly what they wanted. Assuming it was one of those people, she pulled herself up. Instead, she was face to face with a man who looked very much like Santa Claus. Should she press the panic button she had behind the counter? Or grab the mace from her purse?

"Can I help you?" she asked, her hand grasping a knife she kept behind the counter just in case a thief came in and tried to take her money. Although Seagrove was the safest city she'd lived in, she never liked to take chances as a woman alone.

"SuAnn?" The man stared at her, a slight smile on his face. He wasn't bad looking, even if he did resemble the man who lived at the North Pole. He was fairly tall, thin and handsome, if she was being honest. Of course, if he was an ax murderer, none of that would matter.

"Yes. Who are you?"

"You don't recognize me?"

"I don't."

He chuckled. "I suppose it has been a very long time, but I'd know your face anywhere."

She was completely confused. Who was this guy? His voice sounded slightly familiar, low and gruff with an unmistakable southern accent. She trusted people with southern accents more than anyone else.

"Well, don't keep me in suspense," she said, getting more than a little irritated. If there was something SuAnn hated, it was being in the dark about anything.

He walked forward a couple of steps, and she tightened her hand around the knife handle. "Don't worry. I'm not here to hurt you, SuAnn. Quite the opposite, in fact."

Just as she was about to get her answer, Mr. Dearen walked through the door, the bell dinging so loudly that it surprised SuAnn and she dropped the knife onto the tile floor. It made a loud metal noise and startled Mr. Dearen.

"Mornin', SuAnn!" He said the same thing every morning, his big smile - with several missing teeth - on full display. He wore a wool hat, a thick wool coat, and shuffled along with a walker.

"Good morning," she said, pretending she wasn't in the middle of a mystery. Even if she needed help, old

Mr. Dearen wouldn't be in any position to protect her. He could barely make it over to the counter himself.

"One large hazelnut coffee, please," he said, sliding the exact change across the counter, as he always did.

She quickly poured his coffee and handed it to him. "Here ya go. See you tomorrow." As much as she hated to hurry him away, she desperately wanted to know who this Santa Claus looking man was.

He nodded and held the cup up toward the mystery man. "This is good stuff. You should try it!"

"I may just do that," the man said, as Mr. Dearen smiled and left the bakery. Now it was just the two of them again.

There was a long moment of tension in the air before SuAnn couldn't stand it anymore. "Out with it!"

He laughed. "Just as impatient as ever, I see."

"Look, I don't know what kind of prank you're trying to pull, but you're way too old for jokes."

The man smiled again. It was really starting to irritate her. "Susie, you always knew how to cut to the chase."

"Susie? The only person who has ever called me Susie is..."

Her heart felt like it stopped in her chest. The way he said it, the sly smile on his face under that bushy white beard. It couldn't possibly be...

"Is it all coming back to you now?"

"Nicholas?"

"In the flesh!" he said, holding his arms out.

"But, how..."

"You're not an easy woman to find, Susie, but I

never gave up. Been trying to find you for almost a year now. This time at least."

"I haven't seen you in... what... forty years?"

"That's about right, I suppose. That was the last high school reunion I went to."

"Same here."

"You're just as beautiful as you were way back then."

What was she supposed to say to that? Nicholas, or Nicky as she often called him, had been the first great love of her life. They'd dated from ninth grade until after graduation, all the while planning to get married and start a family. But then life got in the way.

First, SuAnn's father had unexpectedly died, leaving her to care for her inconsolable mother and little sister. Nicholas had gone into the Army right after high school and served in the Vietnam War. By the time he came home years later, SuAnn was married and pregnant with Janine. She'd heard he was home, but didn't see him because she knew it would've been too hard.

Years later, at their high school reunion, she'd seen him with his wife, and her heart had broken a little. As much as she wanted him to be happy, he'd been her soulmate as far as she was concerned. After that reunion, she'd never gone to another one, not wanting to see him again. It was just too hard.

Even after her husband died, and she'd remarried, she'd thought about Nicky. Where was he? Was he still married? Could old sparks be rekindled?

"Nicholas, why are you here?" She was still standing on the other side of the counter, wanting to keep a safe distance between them.

"Because I never stopped thinking about you, SuAnn."

She stared at him. "It's been decades, for goodness' sakes! And you're married!"

He shook his head. "Darlin', I was only married for six years. We never even had kids."

"What?"

"But you were married. And then, when your husband died, I didn't figure it was the time to ask you on a date."

"How did you know my husband died?"

"I kept up through friends from school, as best I could anyway. I know Richard died when your girls were still teenagers."

She softened a bit at the mention of her precious husband and father of her girls. Richard had been such a solid figure in all of their lives, and he'd allowed SuAnn to be who she was. After losing him when Julie was just a junior in high school, it had forced her to go to work and raise her girls on her own. Sure, they were older, but they'd needed her more than ever after their daddy had died.

"He was a wonderful husband and father." She didn't know why she suddenly felt the need to defend his honor.

"I'm sure he was."

"There were quite a lot of years between my marriage to Richard and my marriage to Buddy. So, if you were so interested in finding me, why didn't you do it then?"

He sighed. "I got married again. Tricia was her name. She passed away about three years ago."

"I'm sorry to hear that."

"Look, Susie, maybe too many years have passed, but I couldn't keep going through life without checking in on you. And when I did an Internet search and saw you'd opened a bakery in this little town, I decided to take my last shot."

She couldn't help but feel flattered. But decades had passed between them. She wasn't the same girl from high school, and she was sure he wasn't the same boy either.

"I don't know what you want me to say, Nicky."

He smiled, the corners of his weathered eyes turning up like little smiles themselves. "I want you to say you'll go to dinner with me tomorrow night."

She poked her lip out and cocked her head like she was deep in thought. In reality, she was about to bust a gut to say yes.

"Well, I suppose that could be arranged."

Nick laughed. "I'll pick you up right here at seven."

As he turned toward the door, she struggled not to giggle like a schoolgirl. The man she'd dreamed about finding her one day actually had. Maybe second chances weren't just for young people, after all.

* * *

Dixie laid her head on the table. "She hates me."

"I'm sure that's not true!" Julie said, rubbing her back. "She's probably just protective of her daddy. That's all."

Dixie sat up and sighed. "I'm telling you, dinner last night was a disaster. I was so jittery that I burned the pork chops. You know I never burn food!"

Julie sat down beside her. "You've got to calm down,

lady. You're starting to aggravate your tremors." Whenever Dixie got nervous, her left hand shook. It always worried Julie because she didn't want her disease to progress any faster than it had to, and stress was one of the worst things for her health.

"Harry keeps telling me I'm overreacting, but I know when someone doesn't like me. Especially another woman. You know, you can just tell."

"Why don't you talk to her? Clear the air? See what she's thinking?"

"I don't want her to think she's gotten to me, but I might just have to talk to her. Something isn't right."

Julie couldn't help but feel bad for Dixie. She was such an amazing person, and anyone who didn't like her had to have a screw loose. "Why don't you take the rest of the day off? Go get your nails done or something?"

Dixie smiled. "I appreciate it, honey, but I need to keep busy. I think I'm going to go in the storage room and go through that new shipment we got."

"Okay, but if you decide you need to get out of here, I'll mind the store."

"I know you will. You're an excellent business partner, Julie."

She watched Dixie walk into the back room and decided she would go straighten up around the cash register. That area always seemed to get messy with coffee cups and stray pens.

As she walked behind the counter, a woman came in. She hadn't seen her before, but that wasn't unusual since tourists were always breezing through their quaint little town. Christmas time was her favorite time of year because it brought out many people in the holiday spirit. The town square was already decorated for the season, with lit-up garlands wrapped around the light posts, a nativity scene in the park area and lights strung in the trees dotting the area.

"Welcome to Down Yonder Books," Julie said, as the woman entered. She was petite with dirty blond hair that was as simple as it was long. Her mother would've called it stringy, but Julie tried not to judge.

"Thanks," the woman said quietly. She seemed anxious, almost skittish.

"Can I help you find something?"

"No thanks. Just looking."

"Well, I'm Julie if you need anything," she said, smiling. The woman glanced at her name tag for a moment and nodded.

"Thanks."

She watched her walk around, occasionally touching a book and sometimes looking back at Julie. It made her wonder if the woman was planning to rob the place, but she had to believe that wasn't true. Still, she monitored her as best she could just in case she was there for some nefarious reason.

A few minutes later, she walked up to the counter, no books in her hand. "You sell coffee?"

"We sure do. We have French vanilla, hazelnut, pumpkin spice..."

"You don't sell plain coffee?"

Julie smiled. "Of course. What size?"

The woman leaned a bit and looked at the cups. "That small one."

"Coming right up," Julie said. She turned around and poured the coffee as the woman sat down at the table. Julie walked over and set it in front of her. "Are you new in town?"

She nodded. "Just visiting."

"That's on the house, then! Welcome to Seagrove."

She smiled slightly. "Thanks. It's my first time here."

"You're going to love it. Where are you staying?"

"At the motel down on route six."

"Oh, that's quite a way from here."

"Yeah. It was all I could afford. I just came here to see some family."

"I'll tell you what... Why don't you come stay at the inn I own with my husband? We'll charge you the same price, but it's a much nicer place and just over the bridge onto the island."

Her eyes widened. "Really? You'd do that for me?"

"Of course!"

"But you don't even know me."

Julie smiled. "We welcome everyone to Seagrove, and a motel is no place to spend the holidays."

The woman laughed softly. "It isn't a very nice place."

"Then it's settled." Julie picked up a brochure for the inn off the counter and handed it to her. "You go get your things and come on over to The Inn At Seagrove, okay?"

"Are you sure?"

"Absolutely. I just need one thing from you."

She looked a little hesitant. "What's that?"

"Your name?"

The woman chuckled. "Tina. I'm Tina Hobbs."

"Nice to meet you, Tina," Julie said, shaking her hand. "And Merry Christmas."

"Merry Christmas," Tina said, beaming.

CHAPTER THREE

*M*eg held onto her wiggly daughter, keeping her firmly planted on her lap and trying to smile. "Smile, Vivi..." she encouraged, as the photographer tried in vain to get a good family Christmas photo. So far, he'd gotten a picture of Meg chasing Vivi, followed by a photo of Vivi's behind sticking up in the air while she put her hands in the dirt next to the bale of hay they were sitting on.

"Come on, my darling," Christian urged, his thick French accent still so attractive to Meg. She would never tire of hearing him speak, even when it was the most mundane of sentences. She even loved hearing him order fast food at the drive through they went to from time to time. The way he said pickles gave her the chills.

Finally, the photographer caught Vivi looking straight ahead for a split second and snapped the winning photo. Meg had been sure to dress her in a cute red and green plaid dress that flared out and had a black velvet top. She wore white tights and shiny black shoes. Now that she was walking without help, trying to keep her still was like trying to hold a pig that someone had slicked up with oil.

Meg set her down and allowed her to explore the area of the Christmas tree farm where they were taking photos. She couldn't imagine how hard getting a picture with Santa was going to be at the mall next week. She had plans to go Christmas shopping with her mother, her sister and her aunt Janine, and she was really looking forward to it. There was just something about the energy at the mall during Christmastime. The sound of people talking, the music playing in the stores, the smell of the coffee shop and the place that sold those huge cinnamon rolls.

"There's my adorable little niece!" Colleen said as she walked around the corner. Tucker was behind her, as always. Colleen swept Vivi up in the air and spun her around.

"I wouldn't shake her too much. She just had a bunch of cotton candy that her daddy fed her. She's so pumped up on sugar that I worry she'll never fall asleep tonight!"

Christian shrugged his shoulders. "What can I say? I wanted to make her happy!"

Tucker laughed. "That's what we do, right? We like to make the women in our lives happy."

Colleen bumped his shoulder with hers. "Then where's my cotton candy?"

"Hey, Christian, do you mind showing me where you got that cotton candy?" he said, winking at Colleen. As the two men wandered off, the sisters went in the other direction, Colleen holding Vivi.

"Those two are something else," Meg said.

"Yes, they are. It's good to see you like this, sis."

"Like what?" They stopped at a picnic table and sat down. Vivi toddled over to the small playground nearby as both of them watched.

"So happy. You have a real little family now. I'm so proud of you."

Meg smiled. "Thanks. It was a tough time for a while there, but I finally got my feet under me. I've never been happier in my life."

"So, do you think you and Christian will tie the knot?"

"I hope so. He hasn't asked in a long time, though."

"I'm sure he still wants to get married, Meg. You're his world."

"I don't know. I think I might have spooked him a few months ago. I just wasn't in the mental place to say yes back then."

"But you are now?" Colleen asked as she stopped to pet a donkey that the local petting zoo had brought, along with an assortment of rabbits, goats and an adorable pig.

Meg nodded. "I'm more than ready. I can see us building our family, owning a little house..."

"With a white picket fence?" Colleen said, laughing.

"Yes! I want the white picket fence."

"Then tell him, sis. He's probably on pins and needles wondering if you'd say yes now."

Meg reached down to pet a goat. She knew she should talk to Christian and let him know that she was ready to get married, but what if he'd changed his mind along the way? What if he was happy with how things were?

* * *

"Now, you can put the gum drops all along the edge right here. And don't forget to put some icing right there so that the licorice will stick," Julie said as she helped Dylan build his very first gingerbread house.

It reminded her of the days when her girls were young, and they would do all sorts of things around Christmas time. They made memories that would last a lifetime.

Now that she got to see Meg do those things with Vivi, it caused those memories to flood back into her mind. Little did she know a year ago that she would sit at her dining room table, staring into the eyes of her new son, helping him build his very first gingerbread house. All she could hope was that this memory would be something he would think back on one day when he had kids.

"Like this?" Dylan asked, carefully placing the last of the gum drops along the roofline.

Julie smiled and touched his arm. "You really can't mess it up. And you're doing an outstanding job!"

The sun had just set, and Lucy was back in the kitchen preparing dinner. If there was one thing Julie was excited about, it was seeing Lucy back at the inn. She had spent some much needed time with her family, but Julie had missed her food. Not that Julie was a terrible cook, but it also wasn't something she enjoyed doing every single day. With a new little boy in the house who had a ravenous appetite, she felt like she needed to cook all the time.

When it was just her, she could get by on some microwave meals and the occasional home cooked Sunday meal. Plus, Dixie would often bring a lot of the food, so she didn't feel like she was doing it alone. And then when it was her and Dawson just dating, he would often help her cook.

A new little boy with an enormous appetite had proved to be a challenge over Thanksgiving. It seemed like Julie couldn't feed him enough. Every time she turned around, he was asking for a snack or she was making a sandwich. He didn't have a big weight problem, although he was on the chubbier side. She remembered those days herself when she still had baby fat. It all melted off when she became more active in her teenage years.

"Wow! You two are doing a fantastic job with that. Are you having a good time, Dylan?" Dawson asked, as he walked through the door. He had been outside, working on some project in the barn. Julie wasn't sure exactly what it was, but Dawson had taken up an interest in building furniture, so she figured it had something to do with her Christmas present that he was being very tightlipped about.

"It's really fun!" Dylan said, sneaking one of the final gum drops and popping into his mouth. Julie pretended she didn't see him.

"Listen, I need to tell you something. I hope you don't get mad, but a woman came into the bookstore today that really seemed in need. She's visiting town for the first time, says she has some family here. Anyway, she kind of appeared down on her luck, and she was staying over at the motel."

Dawson smiled. "You offered her a room here, didn't you?"

Julie scrunched her nose and shrugged her shoulders. "Are you upset?"

He leaned down and kissed her on top of the head. "Of course not! It's Christmas, and we do for others at Christmas, don't we?"

Dylan nodded. "That's what my Sunday school teacher said. We should do nice things for other people all year, but especially at Christmas time because that's what God would want us to do."

Julie and Dawson had gotten Dylan involved with their church. He needed a foundation, and not just one with his family. They wanted to do everything they could to rebuild his sense of security after suffering so many losses in his young life. They wanted him to have a community of people surrounding him who loved him and would always be there for him.

"We will always welcome people here when we have room," Dawson said.

Dylan giggled. "Like they had to welcome Mary and Joseph at the inn?"

Dawson nodded. "I guess it's a lot like that. Anyway, when is this lady coming?"

"Tonight. In fact, I expect her to show up at any minute."

"Do we know her name?"

"Tina Hobbs."

"I'll go get her room ready. And if you can tell Lucy

that we're going to have an extra mouth to feed for the next little while, that would be helpful."

Julie watched her husband walk up the stairs and was again in awe of his giving nature. Dawson was truly one of those people who would give the shirt right off his back, and she knew he would never be mad about her inviting someone to stay. Still, she hadn't quite started feeling like the inn was also her home. With Janine living at the cabin with Colleen, she sort of felt like a fish out of water sometimes. She loved living at the inn, with its space and beautiful, sweeping views, but in her mind it was still a part of Dawson's family. His heritage. She figured at some point, it would start to feel like her own home too.

Before Julie had a chance to go tell Lucy, she popped her head out of the kitchen. "Dinner will be ready in about fifteen minutes."

"Thanks, Lucy. Listen, do you mind setting an extra place tonight? We have a new guest who should be arriving soon."

"Sure thing," she said, smiling. Lucy never minded another person at the dinner table. She enjoyed meeting everyone and learning their stories.

"Let's get this cleaned up. Why don't you carefully carry the gingerbread house over to the credenza in the living room?"

Dylan looked at her quizzically. "The what?"

Julie laughed. "That long brown table with the sliding doors next to the fireplace. It's called a credenza. We'll display our work of art right there."

"Ohhhh... Okay. Credenzer?"

"Credenza," Julie said, stressing the A at the end.

Just as Dylan left with the house, she heard a knock at the front door. As she opened it, she saw Tina standing there, a nervous smile on her face. She had a simple black duffel bag in her hand and a brown paper bag in the other.

"Tina, so glad you made it! Did you have any trouble finding the place?"

"No, no trouble at all. Is it still okay if I stay here?"

"Absolutely. We're excited to have you. My husband is upstairs getting your room ready, in fact."

Dylan walked over to the door and stood beside Julie. She put her arm around his shoulders. "This is my son, Dylan."

"Nice to meet you, Dylan," she said, smiling. "You're a very handsome young man."

"Thanks," Dylan said before darting off to the kitchen, most likely to sneak some early bites of chicken and dumplings out of Lucy's pot.

"He's a boy of few words," Julie joked. "Come on in."

Tina walked inside and looked around, her head turning from side to side as she took in the place. "Your tree is beautiful."

"Thank you. We had a fun time putting it up. Please, drop your bag here on this chair."

She set her bag down and continued looking around. "Is that a gingerbread house?"

"It sure is. Dylan and I just finished it, in fact."

"Mind if I look?" she asked, softly.

"Of course. Make yourself at home."

Tina walked over and looked at the house, a smile on her face. "My grandma did one of these with me when I was a kid. But this one looks so much better than mine did."

Julie laughed. "Trust me, it looks nothing like the perfect one on the box. But we made some memories, and that's what counts."

Tina nodded. "Yeah, memories are most important."

"Hi there!" Dawson said, coming down the stairs. "You must be our new guest. Tina, right?"

She nodded. "That's right."

"Welcome to The Inn At Seagrove," he said, reaching out his hand.

"Thanks for having me here. I can pay you what I was paying the motel..."

Dawson waved his hand. "We wouldn't dream of it. It's Christmas time, and we're honored to have you stay with us."

Her eyes welled with tears. "I don't know what to say. Nobody has ever been this nice to me."

"Well, you've never been to Seagrove. All the nicest people live here," Dawson said, winking at her. "Come on, let me show you your room. I think you'll love the view of the ocean."

Tina nodded and followed him, but not before Dawson took her bag from her hand. Ever the chivalrous southern man, Julie would never take him for granted. As she watched him disappear up the stairs with Tina following behind him, she had to wonder what life this woman had lived that would make her cry over the kindness of strangers.

* * *

"So, what's the big news?" Janine asked. Colleen had come home from work very excited about something.

"Tucker is getting an amazing opportunity. He's been working on it all week with Jamison O'Malley!"

"You mean the guy who owns the toy company?" Janine asked as she made herself a sandwich for dinner. She had never been a good cook, and not having her sister live there anymore had really cramped her style as far as her food choices went. Tonight's menu was a turkey sandwich with mustard and a side of whatever chips she could find in the back of the pantry.

"The very same one!"

"Is he going to work for him?"

"No. Jamison actually wants to pick up his toy and make it one of the main ones they are going to market in the new year. We didn't quite make the Christmas cut off, but they believe they can build an entire marketing campaign around it for next Christmas."

"That's great! I know Tucker must be excited."

Colleen laughed. "Tucker is a nervous wreck. I'm excited!"

"Yes, Tucker tends to get nervous about these kinds of things. What an amazing accomplishment it would be to have his toy as one of the most popular ones next Christmas."

"I know. Of course, he wishes that it would've been for this Christmas, but it's okay. Any progress is good progress."

Janine leaned against the counter and took a bite of her sandwich, washing it down with a big gulp of sweet tea. "William is nervous because he's going to be in the Christmas boat parade."

"I didn't know there was a boat parade."

"Yeah. The town council asked him to be a part of

it. It's going to be great for his business because he gets to have a big sign on the side of his boat as it moves through the marsh during the parade. But we need to go out and buy all the decorations for it. I think I talked him in to dressing up like Santa Claus and waving at the kids. I'm going to be an elf and throw candy."

Colleen laughed. "Aunt Janine, I love you, but you don't have a powerful arm. How in the world are you going to get candy from the boat all the way over to the side of the marsh where the kids would stand?"

"Let me show you what I got." Janine put her sandwich back on the plate and trotted over to the living room. She reached into a large plastic bag and pulled out a long plastic thing that launched tennis balls for dogs.

"You're going to throw the candy at the children like they're dogs?"

Janine nodded her head. "Kids love candy. They don't care how they get it."

* * *

Dixie sat on the porch, the night air crisp against her skin. Even though it was December, she still couldn't stop wearing her favorite pajamas. But they weren't nearly thick enough. She'd have to move to her flannel PJs soon enough.

When she heard the door open, she was expecting to see Harry standing there. Instead, it was Carrie. For a moment, she looked as though she wanted to back up into the house and pretend she'd never opened the door, obviously having assumed the porch was empty. Instead, she found Dixie sitting there on the swing, her slippered feet pushing off the concrete front porch.

"Come on out. There's plenty of room," Dixie said, always trying to be the friendly host. Her mother had taught her to welcome everyone, especially the ones you really didn't want to welcome. She had been a devout Christian woman, and the strength she'd shown over her lifetime was something Dixie still aspired to at her age.

The last few days of Carrie being there had been difficult, to say the least. She barely uttered five words a day to Dixie, but Harry didn't see it. Not wanting to cause a rift between Harry and his daughter, Dixie had smiled and played along.

"Thanks," Carrie said, stepping out onto the porch with a cup of coffee in her hand. She was still wearing her day clothes, a thick gray sweater and a pair of jeans. She sat down in one of the white wicker rockers Dixie kept on her porch and took a sip of her coffee, warming her hands on the sides of the mug.

"I hope you enjoyed dinner." Dixie had made her famous country fried steak with gravy and homemade biscuits. It was her favorite meal to make, and Harry said it's what kept "meat on his bones" even with Parkinson's.

"It was good. Thanks."

The silence was deafening. Those uncomfortable pauses in conversation had always been hard for Dixie. She liked to hear people talking, laughing, interacting. When it was quiet, she struggled with what to say and do.

"So, any idea how long you plan to stay?"

Carrie looked at her, as if she couldn't believe what she'd just heard. "Is there a time limit?"

Dixie put her hand on her chest. "Of course not. I didn't mean it that way..."

"It sounds like you're ready for me to leave."

Oh, now she'd really stepped in it. "No. Your father is really enjoying you being here."

"Just my father, though, right? I mean, let's be honest, Dixie. You're not enjoying my presence here at all."

Dixie bit her lips, trying not to let her feisty southern side out. That was a part of her personality she tried to keep under wraps unless she was fighting with a bill collector or talking to the IRS. "Carrie, I'd like to be honest with you."

"Please do."

The tension was so thick that Dixie was sure she could cut it with the dullest of butter knives. "I've felt very uncomfortable since you got here."

"Well, at least you're admitting it," she said, her voice monotone.

"And it's not because I didn't want you here. I was quite excited, actually. And nervous. But, since you've been here, I feel anxious in my own home, and that just isn't okay."

"Excuse me?" Again, Carrie looked at her like she'd never had anyone be honest with her in her life.

"Honey, I love your father more than I can describe. I lost my first husband decades ago, and I swore to never marry again. It's not like I didn't have opportunities, you see. But, Harry just gets me. He understands me. He complements me, and I like to think I complement him too. And the one thing I wanted to give him was you."

"Why are you telling me this?"

"Because, for some reason, you can't stand me. I get it. I'm not everyone's cup of tea, but I am your daddy's wife, and I won't be disrespected in my own home."

Carrie scoffed and rolled her eyes before standing up. "Then I'll leave in the morning." She turned toward the door.

"No, please don't. That's not what I'm saying at all." Dixie was so afraid she was going to pack up and take off.

"Then what are you saying?"

"Please, sit back down. Please."

Carrie sucked in a sharp breath and sat back down on the edge of the rocker. "You know, I haven't seen my dad much in the last few years. We had words a few times, and we'd just started rebuilding our relationship when..."

"When I came along?"

She nodded. "Yes."

"Darlin', you're a grown woman. Certainly, you don't worry that I'll take your daddy away from you?"

"No. That's not it."

"Do you think I'm trying to replace your mom? Because I'm not."

"No, I don't think that."

Dixie leaned back. "So, it truly is that you just don't like me?"

Carrie chuckled under her breath. "You are a little much sometimes, with your jewelry and bejeweled sweaters. But, it's not that I dislike you."

"Then what is it?" Dixie asked, throwing her hands in the air.

"I guess I've been holding something against you, and maybe it's not your fault."

"What?"

Carrie set her coffee cup on the wicker table next to her and leaned back in the chair. "I've always wanted to take care of my dad, but we had a rift for a long time. When we worked things out, I finally asked him to come stay with me in California. I bought a house with a guest suite all set up for him. Then, he told me no. Said he'd met a woman who wanted to travel like he did."

"Oh..."

"He's got a disease. I'm worried about him. I want to take care of him, get him the best medical treatment..."

"So, you want him to be your patient?"

"What?"

Dixie smiled. "Carrie, your daddy is still a vibrant man. He'd never want to live with his child and be taken care of like an invalid."

"I didn't call him an invalid!"

"You know him. That's what he'd feel like. Look, we both have Parkinson's. We see skilled doctors here. And we take care of each other. We're living our best lives! Who knows how much time we have left, but at least we'll spend it kicking up our heels and having fun! I mean, we might fall down or fling salt all over the kitchen, but we're living."

Carrie laughed. "You're quite a character, Dixie."

"I'll agree with that. So, can we start over? What do you say?"

"As long as you take care of Dad and always let me see him, I think we can make this work."

Dixie smiled. "Oh, sugar, I would never try to keep you from seeing your daddy! I just want us to be friends, that's all."

"I need another cup of this amazing peppermint coffee. Care for a cup?"

Dixie stood up to follow her into the house. "I need decaf, because the Lord knows I don't need an extra pep in my step before bed!"

CHAPTER FOUR

*J*ulie opened the drapes and allowed the bright sunlight to envelop the living room. She loved early morning, especially now that Dylan was out of school for winter break. The beams of sunlight danced across the hardwood floors, warming them for her son's fast little feet that would run across it soon.

She sat down on the antique sofa - not her favorite - and took her first sip of coffee, her slippered feet resting on the mahogany coffee table in front of her. While she loved the history of her new home, she wasn't a fan of the furnishings. Dawson had kept them because they belonged to his grandmother, so Julie wasn't about to say anything.

"Good morning," Tina whispered as she came down the staircase.

They'd had a nice dinner together the night before, although Tina was definitely quiet. She was one of those people that you could tell had a turbulent history and was trying to get her footing now. Julie found those kinds of people interesting. Maybe it was because she worked in a bookstore, or maybe it was because she was writing her first novel, but she always wondered about those kinds of stories. What made people tick? What complex backgrounds had caused them to become who they were?

So far, all she knew about Tina was that she was in her early thirties, unmarried and was born in north Georgia. She'd worked in a retail store that sold women's clothing for several years, and now she was unemployed.

"Good morning. If you'd like some coffee, I have a pot in the kitchen," Julie offered, starting to stand up.

Tina held up her hand. "No, but thank you. Caffeine gives me migraines."

"Oh, I'm so sorry. I can ask Lucy to brew some decaf..."

"It's fine. Really. But thanks." Tina walked over to the Christmas tree and touched an ornament. "Did Dylan make this?"

Julie laughed. Dylan had made a hand painted snowman ornament at school, but he'd painted each snowball a different color so it looked like the colors for his favorite team. "Yes. Dylan is very into sports."

She turned around and smiled. "He's a cute kid. He must keep you on your toes."

"Oh, he does. To be honest, we just adopted him from foster care a few months ago."

"He seems really happy here."

"I hope so. We adore him. I always wanted a son, and now I have one. So, do you have kids?"

Tina looked uncomfortable, and Julie immediately regretted her question. "I was never blessed to become a mother."

"I'm so sorry I asked you that, Tina. It was none of my business. I hope I didn't bring up any pain..."

She walked to the chair and sat down. "It's okay. Really, it is. It's just that being here with your family has shown me what I've missed out on. As a kid, all I ever wanted to be was a mother. I guess it just wasn't meant to be."

"It's not too late, you know. Plus, there's always adoption. I never thought I'd become a mother again in my mid-forties, yet here I am."

As if on cue, Dylan came bounding down the stairs. He was so full of energy from the time he awoke until Julie forced him to go to bed. She didn't remember her daughters being nearly as energetic as her new son.

"Good morning!" he said, almost yelling.

"Good morning. Inside voice, though," Julie said, smiling.

"Sorry."

"Say good morning to Miss Tina too."

He looked at her and smiled, his missing front teeth his most prominent feature at the moment. "Good morning, Miss Tina."

She smiled. "Good morning, Dylan."

"I think Lucy cooked you some biscuits and bacon in the kitchen."

"Yay!" he shrieked before running through the door to the kitchen. The boy had an appetite, she'd give him that.

"I wish I had his energy," Tina said, laughing.

"Same here. I never realized how exhausting it would be to become a mother again at my age."

"That must be a challenge."

"It is, but he's so worth it."

"Do you mind if I ask what happened to his parents?"

Julie sighed. She didn't want to violate Dylan's privacy, so she decided to just hit the highlights. "His father recently passed away, which landed Dylan in foster care."

"Oh wow. That's so sad. Were they close?"

"Honestly, I don't know much about that, and I've never asked Dylan. If he wants to talk about it, I'm sure he will one day."

"Of course. I didn't mean to pry."

"No worries."

"I assume they contacted Dylan's mother before he went to foster care?"

"I'm not sure. Unfortunately, she left a long time ago, when Dylan was very young."

"Oh. That's terrible. A boy needs his mother."

Julie smiled. "Well, thankfully, he has his mother now. Love is way more important than blood."

Tina nodded. "You're right. I can see he's well loved here."

Dylan came bounding back out of the kitchen, a biscuit in one hand and a piece of bacon in the other. Of course, no napkin.

"Young man, you get back in the kitchen and get a plate. We're not eating like animals around here!" Julie said, pointing him back to the kitchen door. Before he could make it there, Lucy came walking out.

"I told you not to run out there," she said, shaking her head and laughing. "I've never seen a kid get so excited about biscuits and bacon."

She ushered him back into the kitchen.

Julie and Tina both laughed.

"Listen, I'm not sure what you're planning to do today, but I'm going with my daughters and some friends to do a little Christmas shopping at the mall if you'd like to join us." Tina looked surprised. "Really? That would be amazing. I haven't been to the mall in a long time. Of course, I don't really have anyone to buy for this year."

Julie cocked her head a bit. "I thought you said you were here to visit family?"

Tina cleared her throat. "Yes. Extended family, though. Not anyone I would buy Christmas presents for."

"Oh. I see. Well, you're still welcome to join us."

"I'd love to. Maybe it will put me in the Christmas spirit."

* * *

Tucker sat at the table, enjoying a sandwich. Colleen was with her mom and sister doing some Christmas shopping at the mall. A part of him was glad to have a bit of time alone to clear his head.

He was really excited and nervous about the new partnership with Jamison O'Malley. It had grown from one toy to possibly an entire line of toys that would come out during the next Christmas season. Never in his dreams did he think he would have an opportunity for something like that.

But, if he was honest, he was questioning himself.

Was he really ready for this? Was he good enough? What would happen to his name in the toy invention business if everything he created flopped?

"Hello," Christian said, standing in front of him. He was waving his hand in front of Tucker's face.

"Oh, hey, man. Sorry. I didn't see you standing there."

Christian laughed. He towered above Tucker by what seemed like ten feet. Tall and lanky, and with his thick French accent, he stuck out like a sore thumb around Seagrove.

"You looked very lost in thought."

"I was. Please, sit down."

Christian sat down across from him, setting his briefcase on the ground. As a college professor, he always looked the part. Dress pants, a button up dress shirt and even a sweater vest today because it was cold.

"Can I get you anything?" The server said when she walked over to the table.

"Sure. I'll have a Cobb salad and water with lemon."

As the server walked away, Tucker laughed. "No sweet tea?"

"Don't tell Meg, but I still can't get a taste for the stuff. I've tried, believe me."

"I'll keep the secret," Tucker said, laughing.

He enjoyed spending time with Christian. Since they were dating sisters, and would hopefully one day marry them, they might even end up being brothers. Christian was a good guy, and he adored Meg.

"So, I understand the ladies have gone Christmas shopping today."

"Yes, and I shudder to think how many packages

Meg is going to come back with. She doesn't understand that Vivi is a year old and doesn't need fifty presents on Christmas," Christian said, chuckling.

"You two seem very happy."

He nodded his head. "We are. In fact, I don't think I've ever been so happy in my life. The only thing that would make it better is a wedding ring."

Tucker took a sip of his tea. "Then give her one."

"I don't think she wants to get married."

"Yes, she does. She told Colleen..."

Oh, no. What had he just done? In his effort to have an interesting conversation with Christian, he had somehow spilled the beans that Meg wanted him to propose.

"What were you about to say?"

"Nothing. I wasn't about to say anything."

Christian leaned forward, his hands clasped together in front of him. "Tucker, I know you were about to say something. Spill it."

"It's not my place."

Christian stared at him. "Do you mean that Meg told Colleen she wants me to propose?"

"I didn't say that."

Christian squinted his eyes. "But you're not saying that it's not true?"

"I'm getting very lost in this conversation."

Christian leaned back and crossed his arms. "So she wants me to propose?"

"Have you tried their tuna salad here? I hear that it's the best in town."

"Stop trying to change the subject. And, also, you're a terrible liar."

Tucker sighed. "Fine. I didn't mean to say that out loud, but yes. Meg told Colleen that she would like to get married but she's afraid you'll never ask her again."

There. He said it. There was no taking it back now.

"Oh, my goodness. All this time I thought she might never want to get married, and she's just been waiting for me?" The smile on Christian's face was so broad that it practically touched both sides of the town square.

"I guess this is joyous news?"

Christian laughed. "Oh, yes, this is great news. But we must keep it a secret that I know."

Tucker shrugged his shoulders. "Of course. I'm great at keeping secrets."

* * *

SuAnn couldn't stop smiling. Since her dinner the other night with Nicholas, her cheeks had been hurting. He'd taken her to a wonderful Italian restaurant over in Charleston. Sitting on the veranda near the water, the Spanish moss-covered trees offering beautiful views of the orange and purple sunset, it had felt like a fairy tale.

They'd walked along the water after dinner, reminiscing about old times, and it seemed like no time had passed. SuAnn hadn't felt this way in decades. Having Nicholas there felt like finding her favorite stuffed animal from childhood. The comforting feeling was hard to describe, which was exactly why she hadn't told her daughters.

Now she was at the mall with them, Dixie and some stranger named Tina that had managed to get an invitation. She didn't care much for new people, especially ones that seemed to be mooching off her daughter and Dawson.

"What do you know about this woman, anyway?" She asked Julie as they stood in line for coffee.

"She's down on her luck, Mom. It's Christmas. We're just helping her out."

"Well, you'd better give her a deadline to get out, or else you'll have one of those cases I see on the court TV shows."

They moved up a spot in line. "Oh, good Lord, Mom. Relax."

"I'm serious, Julie. They're called squatters, and you have to move heaven and earth to get them out of your house!"

Julie rolled her eyes. "Let's change the subject. Janine and I would both like to know where you've been lately?"

"What do you mean?" SuAnn asked, trying to sound nonchalant. Having daughters meant that she could get nothing past them. What was it about women that allowed them to sense things that men didn't? It really was a superpower.

Julie looked at her and laughed. "You've always been a terrible liar, Mom. We know something's up. Besides, you're getting new wrinkles from smiling so much. And pardon me for pointing out the obvious, but you've never been someone who smiled a lot."

"Thanks a lot!"

"It's not a put-down, Mom. It's just that you normally have more of a... scowl on your face."

"Julie! What a terrible thing to say to your mother."

They moved to the front of the line and ordered their drinks. Julie got her regular peppermint chocolate mocha with whipped cream on top, and SuAnn ordered a white chocolate latte with light foam. Nothing ever changed.

As they sat at one of the tables waiting for their drinks, Julie continued to press her.

"All I'm saying is that it seems like you're happier lately, and we'd love to know why and celebrate that with you."

"Or make fun of me," SuAnn said under her breath.

Julie reached over and touched her arm. "Mom, we wouldn't make fun of you for being happy. It's okay to feel good about your life, you know."

"Okay, fine. When I was in high school, there was a boy named Nicholas. We were very much in love and planned to get married, but things just didn't happen the way we thought they would."

"I never knew you had a high school sweetheart. Why didn't you tell me?"

"Because I married your father, and there was no use in bringing it up."

"So he contacted you?"

SuAnn couldn't help but smile again. Stupid happiness kept overtaking her poker face.

"He did more than contact me. He showed up at the bakery out of the blue, and we went to dinner the next evening in Charleston."

Julie grinned. "That's amazing!"

"He's so wonderful, but it all seems too good to be true."

"Mom, you deserve something great to happen. Are you in love with him?"

"Well, I used to be. But we're older now, and I'm sure we've both changed. We're going to take it slow."

"That's a good idea. I'm thrilled for you."

She looked into her daughter's eyes and saw honesty. She was genuinely happy for her.

"Can I ask you something?"

"Sure," Julie said, craning her head to check for their coffee order.

"Would it bother you if I said Nicholas was my soulmate?"

"Why would that bother me?"

"Because of your father."

"Mom, I know you loved Dad. But that doesn't mean he was your soulmate, and that's okay. You might have the chance of a lifetime here to reconnect with the man you were always supposed to be with. Don't feel guilty or weird about that."

SuAnn smiled yet again. "Thank you, Julie. You know, you and I have really come a long way."

"We sure have."

"I'm still worried about this Tina woman..."

"Oh, Mom," Julie said, rolling her eyes and shaking her head.

* * *

"Aren't these adorable?" Meg said, holding up a tiny pair of pink cowboy boots. "Vivi is going to have a fit over these!" She added them to her pile of goodies as she walked toward the register.

"Christian is going to strangle you," Colleen said with a laugh. "Vivi's room isn't big enough for all this stuff!"

"Our apartment is getting a little cramped. But come on. Look at this doll. She is going to be so excited when she sees it!"

Meg couldn't help herself. Now that Christian was making good money at the college, and she had her extra income working for one of her professors, she finally felt free enough to spend a little on her daughter.

"Darlin', that baby girl will remember none of this stuff, but you sure are when you get that credit card bill in January!" Dixie said in her larger-than-life kind of way.

"Fine. I'll put back the yellow dress... and the tap shoes..."

"Tap shoes?" Julie said as she walked up with Tina. The two of them had gone to look at some particularly amazing candles. "Vivi doesn't know how to tap dance, Meg!"

Meg grinned. "But wouldn't she look so cute learning?"

Janine rolled her eyes. "Oh, goodness. Somebody take her wallet away."

As the women laughed, even at her expense, Meg was so grateful in that moment. She was surrounded by strong women who loved her, and most people couldn't say they were so blessed.

"Okay, let me pay for all of this and then can we eat some lunch?"

"Yes! I'm starving," Julie said, putting her hand on her stomach.

"I'll just meet y'all after you eat," Tina whispered.

"What? No way! You're eating with us, lady!" Dixie said. "We treat our guests like family, and I'm buying your lunch today. I won't take no for an answer."

Tina looked at Julie. "Trust me, she won't. You might as well let her do it."

"Thank you so much, Dixie. I swear, the people in this town are the nicest I've ever met," she said, a broad smile on her face.

"Just don't take advantage of that," SuAnn muttered under her breath. If Tina heard her, she didn't react, but Meg elbowed her grandmother.

"Stop it," she mouthed, almost dropping some of her items. Sometimes, she didn't know what was in her grandmother's head.

"Pay for that stuff, Meg. We're going to starve to death," Colleen prodded.

"I told y'all to bring a snack..." Meg said as she walked away. She heard them all grumble and couldn't help but smile.

CHAPTER FIVE

*D*awson hammered in the last nail and then lifted the large structure over onto William's boat. When he had heard that his friend was entering the Christmas boat parade, he assumed he was going to be helping him hang some garland and lights around the edge of the boat. Instead, he'd spent the last two hours building a platform that Janine and Julie would decorate. Apparently, William was going to dress up like Santa Claus and throw candy at the kids.

"Man, that thing is heavy!" Dawson said, wiping the sweat from his brow.

"Thanks so much for doing this. There's no way I could build all of this stuff without your help. Besides, everybody knows you are the master at carpentry," William said laughing.

"You don't have to butter me up. I'm already here working."

"So, Janine tells me you have some lady staying at the inn now?"

"Yeah. Julie met her at the bookstore and felt bad for her. Her name is Tina."

"What's she like?"

"Honestly, I don't know too much about her. She seems nice enough, but very guarded. Pretty quiet. I think she's had kind of a rough go at life."

"It's nice of y'all to let her stay. How's Dylan doing?"

"Crazy and energetic as ever," Dawson said, chuckling. "But, you know, he's everything I've ever wanted in a son. I don't feel like he's adopted. He feels like my own biological child."

"Blood means nothing. It's all about family loving each other," William said as he started sanding the edge of the wooden platform.

"You should write greeting cards," Dawson said, teasing him.

"Janine and I have talked about adoption."

"Really, I wouldn't have predicted that."

"With Janine's age, it's unlikely that we could have biological children, and it's not that important to us. But we might check into the foster care system after seeing what amazing results y'all have had."

"That's great. I hope you get to do that. It has been a blessing for us."

"Of course, we would have to get married."

"Well, it's not totally necessary, but it's preferable."

"To us it's necessary. You know those good old southern values," William said, smiling.

"So, do you think you'll pop the question soon?"

"Maybe. Not right now, though. Things are so hectic at the yoga studio and with this new charter business that I'd like to stash some money away before doing that."

Dawson looked at him. "Man, if you're trying to wait for things to be perfect, that's never going to happen. Don't want to butt into your business, but if you love her, there's no reason to wait."

William nodded. "I'm sure you're right. I guess I'm just waiting for the perfect moment."

"Well, you could do like we did and get engaged at your own wedding."

William laughed. "You two are very unique, for sure."

"Are y'all working or talking?" Janine asked as she walked down the dock and over to the boat.

"Don't judge us. We've been working our rear ends off all day," Dawson said, pointing at her, his eyes squinting.

William stepped out of the boat and gave her a hug, kissing the top of her head before returning to his work.

"This platform looks amazing!"

"Yeah, it was a bear to build, but I think it's going to suit what you'll need."

"Thanks so much for doing this. William, I brought you some lunch if you're hungry." She leaned in and put a small cooler on the floor of the boat.

"Thanks, honey," he said, winking at her.

"Sorry I didn't bring you anything, Dawson. I wasn't sure that you'd still be here."

"No worries. I'm about to head out, anyway. I promised Dylan that I would help him write a letter to Santa Claus this afternoon."

Janine smiled. "I love seeing you as a father,

Dawson."

"Well, I love being one."

"Don't let me hold you up, man," William said. "I know you have things to do back at the inn."

Dawson smiled. "Yeah, I'm making something really special for Julie for Christmas."

"I heard you had a big secret project," Janine said.

Dawson stepped up onto the dock. "I do, and I think she's going to love it. At least I hope she does!"

* * *

"A cookie party?"

"Yes. I used to do this with my girls when they were young, so I thought it would be fun to do it again with Dylan and Vivi. You know, start a new tradition?"

Dixie smiled. "Darlin', I think that is a fabulous idea."

Julie recalled the days when her daughters were small and they would throw a big party at Christmas time. They would invite family and friends to bring plain sugar cookies, and then Julie would supply icing and other decorations. They would turn on Christmas music, light a fire, and decorate cookies for hours. At the end, they would pack up most of the cookies and deliver them to local fire stations.

Not only had it taught her daughters about giving to others, but it had given them lifelong memories of spending Christmas with everyone they loved.

"I'm sure our local fire station will be pleased to get a bunch of cookies. Those guys work so hard for the community!"

"Yes, they do. I can't wait to plan this party. I think Colleen and Meg will be excited too."

Dixie stacked the disposable cups beside the coffee machine. "Carrie and I are supposed to make fruitcakes together this afternoon."

"Sounds like you two are making strides in your relationship?"

"Somewhat. It comes and goes," Dixie said, opening a roll of quarters and dropping them into the cash register. The old register needed to be updated desperately, but Julie hadn't talked Dixie into buying a new one.

"What do you mean?"

"We get along better now, but there are moments I feel like she pulls back a bit. Of course, my personality can be a little much I suppose."

Julie laughed. "No. Not possible."

"We're going to make fruitcakes for the Christmas festival. From what I understand, Carrie has never cooked much, so this ought to be interesting."

"And you're starting her out on fruitcakes, of all things?" Julie said, laughing as she removed some books from one shelf and replaced them with newer ones. One thing she'd learned about working in a bookstore was that nothing was static. There were always new books coming, and the older books had to make way for them. Those that didn't sell well got thrown onto the clearance table and then donated.

Since she was slowly working on her first novel, she wondered if her book would be one of the ones that survived or would end up with a big red sticker, lying on a clearance table, begging someone to read it.

"Oh, fruitcake isn't that hard. Plus, I'll be right beside her."

The front door chimed as SuAnn walked into the

store. She rarely came to Down Yonder because she was so busy at her bakery.

"Mom, what are you doing here? Is everything okay?"

"Why would something be wrong?" She asked.

"You normally don't come down here."

"Well, this is a bookstore, Julie. Maybe I just need a book?"

Dixie laughed. "We sure have plenty of those. Can I interest you in a book on Kama Sutra?"

"Dixie!" Julie said, her mouth dropping open. She tried not to laugh, but she couldn't help it.

"The woman has a new boyfriend. I'm just trying to be helpful. Just because we're old doesn't mean..."

"Please," Julie said, holding up her hand.

SuAnn chuckled. "I might grab a copy of that one, Dixie. But, for now, I just wanted to get a cookbook."

"A cookbook? What kind of cookbook?" Julie asked. Her mother had never been a skilled cook. She was a wonderful baker, but the cooking part had been hit or miss over the years. She remembered many impossible to chew pot roasts from her childhood.

"French cooking."

"French cooking? Since when did you get an interest in that?"

SuAnn almost looked like she was about to blush. "Fine. Nicholas loves French food. He was stationed there at one time. I would like to make him beef bourguignon with garlic mashed potatoes and maybe even a baguette."

"Oh my gosh, this is so adorable..." Julie said under her breath.

"Now, don't you be making fun of your momma. The possibility of falling in love at our age is right up there with getting struck by lightning or being run over by a stampede of rogue sheep!" Dixie sure had a way with words.

"I think it's wonderful," Julie said, squeezing SuAnn's shoulder. "But, why don't you let Christian teach you? I'm sure he knows how to make all of that more authentically than a book."

SuAnn shook her head. "He's a nice boy, but I can't understand a word he says. I just want to do this in the peace of my own kitchen." Since moving to Seagrove, SuAnn had found a great rental cottage near the square that allowed her to walk to work. It was a good thing because it kept her from needing a car. She was one of the worst drivers Julie knew.

"I know of some great books in the cooking section. Follow me, SuAnn" Dixie said, leading her toward the back of the store.

As Julie watched the two of them disappear behind several shelves of books, she marveled at their improving relationship with each other. They hadn't been friends at the beginning. More than that, she was so happy that each of them had found love and new beginnings in the golden years of their lives. Sometimes, her heart felt like it might explode when she thought about all the ways her life and the lives of those she loved had changed just because she was brave enough to take a leap of faith, move to an unknown place and start her life again. It made her proud.

* * *

Dawson sat down at the dining room table next to

Dylan. "What're you doing?"

"Drawing a picture of my family," he said.

"That's really nice. Is that a tree?" Dawson asked, pointing at a tall skinny thing with four limbs.

"No, Daddy, that's you, silly!" Dylan said, giggling.

"Oh... Good job, son!" He loved calling him son. When he'd lost his child so many years ago, he never thought he'd have another son to love. God had surely blessed him.

"I wanted to send this picture with my letter to Santa Claus so he'd know where I live now."

"Good idea."

"I'm sorry to interrupt," Tina said as she came downstairs. "I was just going to make myself a cup of tea, if that's okay."

Dawson smiled. "Tina, we want you to think of this place as your own while you're here. You are free to do whatever you need."

She nodded. "Thank you again for your hospitality." She walked over to the tea cart that Julie had set up and pressed the button to heat up the electric kettle. Julie kept a large assortment of tea bags on hand for guests. She had everything from peppermint to more exotic flavors like ginger-orange.

"Care for a gingerbread muffin with your tea?" Dawson asked, holding up a basket full of the delectable treats Lucy had made for the guests.

"Sure. Thanks," she said, taking one from the basket.

"Please, join us."

Tina sat down and took a bite of the muffin. "Wow. This is amazing."

"Lucy is a genius in the kitchen," Dawson said, taking a muffin for himself.

"She made me blueberry pancakes this morning with crunched up bacon in them," Dylan said, licking his lips.

"Oh, that sounds very good." Tina blew on her tea and then took a sip.

"Did you enjoy shopping with the ladies the other day?"

"I did. They are a fun group. Julie has been so welcoming to me. Honestly, I thought I might end up alone for Christmas, so this has been a blessing to me."

Dawson hadn't heard her say that many words since she'd been there, so he was glad she was finally talking.

"Dawson?" Lucy called from the kitchen.

"Excuse me for a moment."

He pushed open the door and saw Lucy standing in a pool of water beside the dishwasher. "Guess what's wrong?" she said, her hands on her hips.

"Oh, no..."

"Should I go get your toolbox?"

"Yes, please."

Dawson walked back to the dining room. "Dylan, I know we were supposed to write your letter to Santa, but I have a mess in the kitchen. Can we do it tonight?"

Dylan poked out his lip. "But, I wanted to get it in the mailbox today. What if it doesn't make it there in time?"

"I don't mind helping him," Tina suddenly said.

"You don't have to do that."

She smiled. "It would be fun. I mean, as long as Dylan is okay with it?"

Dylan grinned. "Yes!"

Dawson laughed. "Okay, but don't ask for a Ferrari or anything, okay? I hear Santa is economizing these days."

"What's a Ferrari?"

"Nevermind."

* * *

Tina had never been around kids much. As an only child, she'd never had the experience of being around them, and babysitting had never been her thing.

"And what else do you want?"

"I want an Army set with the little guns too."

"Are your parents okay with that?"

"It only matters what Santa says I can have, Miss Tina," he said, rolling his eyes and laughing.

"Right. Okay, what else?"

"A puppy."

"I don't think your parents are going to be okay with a puppy running through the inn."

"If Santa says it's okay..."

"Point taken. Okay, what else should we add?"

"Do you think it's okay to add prayers?"

"Prayers?"

"I want to ask Santa to pray for my daddy."

"Your daddy in the kitchen?"

"No. My first daddy. He died."

Tina felt her breath catch in her throat. "I heard about that. I'm really sorry, Dylan. You must miss him."

"Sometimes I do. He liked Christmas a lot. One time, we made cookies. My mom said we're making cookies this year."

"You have a great mom, huh?"

"Yep."

"I'm sorry you lost your first mom and dad, but you have wonderful new ones and that's great."

"I didn't know my first mom, so I don't really miss her."

Tina swallowed hard. "Oh. Well, I'm sure Santa will be happy to say a prayer for your first daddy."

"Okay. Let's put that in the letter too."

* * *

Carrie stood in the kitchen, staring at all the ingredients spread across Dixie's counter.

"All of this is going into the fruitcake?"

"Yes, it is!" Dixie said, pulling out her favorite silicone bakeware.

"Isn't this overkill?"

"Honey, when you taste it, you'll know it was worth all this work. Plus, we're going to take some to the firefighters."

"Okay, what can I do?"

"Grab that bottle of dark rum from the shelf over there."

"I already like this better," Carrie said, laughing.

Dixie loved to hear her laugh because it meant their relationship was getting better and better.

"How's it going in here, ladies?" Harry asked as he walked into the kitchen to pour himself a cup of coffee.

"We haven't even gotten started yet," Dixie said.

"Well, when I get back from my doctor's appointment, I sure hope you'll have it ready for a taste testing."

"We'll try, Dad," Carrie said, rolling her eyes.

Harry quickly hurried out the door as Dixie refocused on making the fruitcakes.

"Now, I've already soaked some dried fruit in the rum overnight, so let me get the dish from the refrigerator."

"You soaked it?"

"It helps break some of the sweetness and gives it a really rich flavor."

"Huh. Never thought of doing that."

Dixie smiled. "Decades of cooking experience in this crazy brain of mine."

"So we put the soaked dried fruit into the batter?"

"Right. And we'll add some orange zest and orange juice to give it some extra flavor."

"And these cut up apples?"

"Yep. And some slivered almonds and chocolate chips."

Carrie laughed. "Sounds like everything you had in the pantry."

"Pretty much!"

"Want to turn on some Christmas music?"

Dixie smiled. "That would make it perfect!"

Carrie fiddled with her fancy phone and turned on some Christmas music as they worked side by side in the kitchen. Dixie couldn't remember a time when she'd had so much fun with someone she barely knew.

Just as they were putting the first two fruitcakes into the oven, someone rang the doorbell. Dixie wiped her hands on her red apron and walked to the door.

"Hey, Mom," William said.

"Hey, sweetie. What're you doing here?"

"Well, I was hoping you might have some decorations up in the attic that I could use on the boat?"

"I'm sure I do. Come on in!"

William walked into the foyer and immediately stuck his nose in the air. "I smell rum. You're making fruitcake?"

"Of course!"

"Got any ready?" He asked, hopefully.

She put her hands on his chest. "No, darlin'. Just went in the oven. But, I want you to come meet your new stepsister."

William followed her into the kitchen. Carrie was busy mixing the rum-soaked fruit with batter, her hair falling out of the messy bun atop her head. One raisin was precariously stuck to her apron.

"Carrie? This is your step-brother, William."

She smiled. "Nice to meet you. I'm Carrie."

He shook her hand and then looked at his. "I can see you've been helping Mom."

She laughed. "Sorry about that."

"It's nice to meet you. Don't let her push you around in the kitchen, though."

"She's teaching me a lot," Carrie said, wiping her hands on a cloth.

"Well, I won't keep y'all. I'm entering my boat in the Christmas boat parade through the marsh. Hoping Mom has some extra decorations in the attic."

"As you can see, I've done plenty of decorating around here, so you are welcome to whatever's up there, son."

He leaned down and kissed her head. "Thanks. Let me know when one of those cakes is ready for a taste tester."

As William walked off, Carrie looked at Dixie. "Hmmm.... Where have we heard that today?"

CHAPTER SIX

ulie sat at the kitchen table, a mound of garland, flowers and other decorations covering the entire tabletop. She was exhausted. Between working full time at the bookstore and helping with the town's Christmas festival, she felt like she was in over her head. This time of the year was supposed to be about joy and fun, but she was stressed today trying to get it all done.

Dawson had helped where he could, but he was busy helping William, running the inn and building her super secret Christmas present out in the barn. She was having a heck of a time keeping her eyes open, even though it wasn't nearly bedtime yet. All she wanted to do was curl up under her fluffy blanket, drink some chamomile tea and drift off into a nice, long slumber.

"Wow! That is a lot of greenery. What are you doing?" Tina asked. She walked over and sat down, setting her a cup of coffee on the table.

"Well, I somehow got myself roped in to making

Christmas wreaths to sell at the festival. The town wants to use the money we raise to go toward the toy drive."

"That's a wonderful thing to do. I'm so amazed at this little town and how everybody seems to help each other. It feels like I landed at the north pole, without all the snow."

Julie laughed. "Make no mistake, there's a lot of hard-working people behind the scenes. But it's a wonderful place. Before I moved here, I didn't have any idea that a place like this existed outside of those sappy TV movies, anyway."

"Where did you move here from?"

"The Atlanta suburbs. I had been married for twenty-one years, and then my husband made a series of poor decisions. Next thing I knew, I was starting my life over here. It turned out to be the best thing that ever happened to me."

"That's amazing. You're a very strong woman to be able to start over like that. I wish I could."

It surprised Julie that she had said something about her history. Both she and Dawson had been careful not to ask too many questions, assuming that if Tina wanted to open up, she would.

"It's never too late to start over, Tina."

She sat there for a moment, her eyes looking lost in thought. "I wish I could believe that, but I've made some terrible choices in my life. I've hurt some people I dearly loved. It just feels like there's no coming back from some of those choices. Maybe I'm meant to be punished, you know?"

"Listen, I don't know what you've been through, but

I know that a new life starts with a new choice. Sometimes, we put ourselves in these self-imposed prisons. If you made bad choices, you have to learn how to forgive yourself. Once you know better, you do better, right?"

Teary-eyed, Tina nodded. "Thank you. I will give that some thought when I say my prayers tonight before bed."

"Can you say a little prayer for me? Because I don't know how in the world I'm going to make twenty-five Christmas wreaths by myself."

Tina laughed. She reached over and pulled some greenery toward her. "You will not do it alone."

"You don't have to help me. You're a guest here!"

"It's the least I can do. And, I have worked at a flower shop before. Do you know how many wreaths I've made in my lifetime?"

Julie stared at her, wide-eyed. "Oh, God has sent me an angel straight from heaven then!"

* * *

"You want me to sing? Christian, come on. You've heard me sing in the car. I swear cats were following us the last time I belted out a Broadway tune."

Christian laughed. "Darling, it's Christmas caroling. Nobody's asking you to stand on a stage and sing an aria. But the Christmas festival requires all of us to contribute something, and certainly we can both stand in a group of people and sing a few Christmas songs."

Meg sighed. She cut up the rest of the banana she had on her plate and slid it over to Vivi, who was sitting in the highchair, waiting for yet another snack. She was a bottomless pit lately. "Fine, but if I get made fun of by my family for the rest of my life, I'm blaming you!"

Christian laughed and then kissed the top of her head. "Your voice is beautiful to me, my love."

She rolled her eyes. "You shouldn't lie. I might be good at a lot of things, but singing is certainly not one of them. Hopefully, everybody else will just drown me out."

"One more thing," Christian said, smiling like he was worried she might fling a dinner plate across the room at him.

"What?"

"We have practice in an hour."

She stared at him. "Tonight? But I just got home from school and Vivi needs a bath..."

"No worries. Your mother said we could drop her by the bookstore for an hour while we do a little practicing on the square."

Meg stood up and poked her finger in the center of his chest, looking up at him. "You're going to get coal in your stocking."

Christian pulled her into a tight embrace, her cheek pressed against his chest, the thumping of his heart loud in her ear. There was no place she would rather be on earth. They had had a rough road at the beginning, first falling madly in love in France and then finding out she was pregnant. There were so many times when Meg thought they would end up apart, but they were stronger than ever now.

"I think Santa will forgive me."

She looked up at him. "I think this is the happiest I've ever been."

He smiled. "I know it's the happiest I've ever been. I

can't wait to spend this Christmas with you, Meg. It's going to be our best one yet."

As she hugged him tightly, she wondered if they would ever make things official. Or would he be one of those guys who never thought he needed to marry her now that they had already started a family? Maybe she had to ask him. Maybe she needed to be honest about her feelings.

For now, she was just going to enjoy Christmas with her new little family and worry about the future another day.

* * *

Colleen stood in the middle of the office, looking from one side of the room to the other. While their offices weren't that big, she never expected so many toys to be delivered.

"And you say there's more coming?" Tucker asked.

"From what I understand. I mean, this is great for the toy drive, but how are we supposed to work here now?"

Tucker laughed. "Why don't we put all of this in the conference room? All future deliveries can go directly there."

"Good idea."

They spent the next half hour moving stacks and stacks of toys into the small conference room. When they were finished, toys were stacked on the table all the way up to the ceiling.

Colleen loved that Tucker was so invested in making sure the less fortunate children in their community had plenty of toys to play with. A big kid at heart, she enjoyed seeing him look at every single donation. Sometimes it appeared as if he was toying with the idea of pulling each item out and playing with it himself, but he refrained.

"So, did Christian tell you he wants all of us to sing at the festival?"

"Yeah, he told me. I tried to explain that I can't carry a tune in a bucket, but that French accent can convince you to do anything," Tucker said, shaking his head.

"Well, then I guess I should hope that no French women get near you," Colleen said, putting her hands on his cheeks. He leaned down quickly and kissed her.

"No woman, French or not, could hold a candle to you."

"Are you just gunning for a really great Christmas present?" she asked, scrunching her nose.

"I already have the best present I could ever have," he said, squeezing her tightly.

"I think you've been around Christian too much. That was super sappy!" she groaned.

As they stood there laughing, Colleen was so thankful. There was nothing else she would've wanted in her life other than what she already had. Some people didn't get to live the life of their dreams, but somehow she was getting to live hers.

Sometimes she thought back to her life in California as an attorney and wondered how she had ended up in a small town in South Carolina working for a toy inventor. Things had really changed in such a short time, but she wouldn't have had it any other way.

"Excuse me? Is this where I'm supposed to drop off a toy donation?"

Colleen looked up and saw Tina standing there holding a small plastic bag.

"Oh, hi, Tina! I'm Colleen. I was at the mall when we went shopping."

"I remember you. Julie's daughter, right?"

"Right. We didn't have time to talk much, but I'm glad you could join us."

"Me too. It was a lot of fun. Julie told me about the toy drive, so I went to buy something I could donate. It's not much, but hopefully it will help," she said, holding out the bag.

"Any donation is welcome," Tucker said, offering up his most genuine smile.

"I wish I could do more. I know these kids need toys for the holidays. It's just a little toy car, but I hope one of them will enjoy it."

Colleen was struck by how quiet and almost sad she seemed. Christmas time in Seagrove was magical, with all the lights and sounds and decorations. All of that was right behind where Tina was standing, but she seemed like a lost soul. Colleen could see why her mother had taken her in for the holidays.

"Some little kid is going to really love this car. I can promise you that," Tucker said.

"Well, I better get back. I've been helping your mom make Christmas wreaths for the festival."

"I'm sure she really appreciates that! She's not the most crafty person I know," Colleen said, laughing.

Tina waved goodbye and walked out the door, pretty much as quietly as she had walked in.

"She seems really sad," Tucker said.

"I know. I can't quite put my finger on it, but I think

she must've had a really difficult past. I mean, she was staying at the worst motel in the area. I just hope she has a good Christmas."

"Me too. Hopefully she finds that the magic of Seagrove will change her life like it has for so many other people."

* * *

Janine stood on the platform of the boat. She knew that Dawson was a great woodworker, but she sure hoped that his handiwork withstood the entire boat parade or she was going to fall in front of everybody.

Dressed as an elf, she was standing next to William, who was all made up as the perfect Santa Claus. It had taken some negotiation to get him to agree to dress up, but he finally relented for the good of the children in the community.

With everybody's help, they had gotten the boat to look as festive as possible, and she was sure that he had a great chance of winning the competition. Even though he got nothing special, other than a Christmas stocking with "first place" embroidered on it, it was the principle of the matter. Any time William did something, he wanted to be the best at it.

They covered the boat in garland and tinsel and all things Christmas. Of course, they had made it a beach theme as well by painting some plastic crabs red and green and peppering them throughout the decor.

It was much like a moving department store window that one would see in a big city. Except this one was floating on water. As they came around the bend, she could see that the crowds that had formed on all the little docks that were dotting the shoreline.

"Do you have the candy ready?" she asked William. He was having a hard time maneuvering himself much, what with the big pillow belted around his midsection. Always in good shape, she found it funny to see him look so portly.

"I've got it. You've asked me that three times," he said, shaking his head.

"Well, I'm sorry. There're dozens of little kids up there who would be very sad if you didn't throw some candy at them."

William laughed. "This is supposed to be fun, Janine. Put a smile on your face and stop worrying so much."

She knew he was right. All the yoga in the world didn't help her when she was under a stressful situation. She could meditate until the cows came home, but anytime she did something outside of her normal box, she got anxiety. It was just a part of the fabric of who she was.

"Look at them. All those grinning faces and people waving."

William raised up his white gloved hand and started waving back at the crowd. Every so often he would yell out "ho ho ho" in his deepest voice. It made Janine giggle, but she turned her head.

"Merry Christmas!" she yelled as they passed the first part of the crowd. She tossed a handful of red and white curved candy canes into the crowd, hoping most of them didn't fall to the ground and shatter at the feet of the children.

She could see Julie and Dawson waving and grinning.

Of course Dylan was right up at the water's edge trying to catch all the candy he could. He had his old Halloween container in his hand and was steadily grabbing pieces as the boat went by and tossing them into the bucket.

She could see her mother waving as well as Dixie and Harry. There were just so many faces she recognized in the crowd, and it made her happy. The people of Seagrove had become her extended family.

All of those years of traveling around the world teaching yoga, Janine had been searching for something. Part of it was searching for herself and who she really was. But the other part had been searching for an anchor. Roots. A place where she felt like she was at home. Seagrove was that place, and the people in it meant more to her than anything in the world.

As she watched William continue to yell ho ho ho and Merry Christmas over and over, she marveled at how much he had changed since she'd met him. When he had first come back to town, he was at odds with his mother and really conflicted within himself. There were so many things that he was holding in and not dealing with, but now he was more open and honest than ever. He seemed happy. Running his own business and being outdoors had changed him in ways she had not expected.

They spent more time together, often out on the boat, winding their way through the marshes full of seagrass and local wildlife. They studied the flora and the fauna and kept their eyes open for alligators, of course. Some of her happiest moments had been out on those marshes with William, the sun setting in the distance and providing a spectacle of orange and pink in the sky.

For the next thirty minutes, they wound their way through the marshes, waving at people and throwing candy before finally coming to the end. When they pulled up to the dock and stopped the boat, William sighed with relief.

"So, do you think we did enough to win this thing?"

She took off her elf hat and kicked off the curly shoes, moving her toes around since they had been way too small. "I think we have a great chance. That was a lot of fun!"

He unbuttoned his Santa suit and pulled the pillow out, waving his hand in front of his stomach to get a breeze. "Never let me get that chubby. I didn't know how hard that would be."

Janine laughed. "Don't worry. You're dating a yoga instructor, so I will always make sure to keep you flexible and lean."

He smiled and pulled her into a hug, leaning down to kiss her cheek. "Thanks for being my elf today."

"No problem, Santa."

* * *

Tina had decided not to go to the boat parade. Today, she was just feeling a little melancholy. Christmas was coming, and she longed so much to have a family of her own to share it with. She relished the alone time this morning while everyone was at the parade so she could wallow in her feelings.

As she watched Julie and Dawson maneuver life with their new son, Julie's daughters and even a grandchild, she sometimes wished that she'd made different choices in her younger years.

She sat at the dining room table, making yet another wreath to help Julie with the Christmas festival. She didn't mind doing it. In fact, she had always enjoyed crafts.

When she was a little girl, her grandmother used to do all kinds of things like this with her. She taught her to sew, how to arrange flowers and even how to bake. When she had died, Tina was only in middle school, and she had missed her grandmother's influence in her life ever since then.

She hadn't been so blessed to have a wonderful mother and father. Her mother had been an alcoholic since Tina was a baby and had died when Tina was seventeen, and her father had never been in the picture. As an only child, it had left her feeling very lonely growing up.

When she had decided to visit Seagrove, she had second-guessed her decision multiple times. She knew it probably wasn't been the right thing to do. She knew that she was telling a lot of lies to a lot of people. But she just couldn't help herself.

Christmas had always been the saddest day of the year for her, and now she was getting to experience what it was like to be with an actual family at the holidays. When everything was over, she didn't know how she would ever leave.

But surely if these people knew her past and what kind of person she really was, they would throw her suitcase out by the curb before she could even say Merry Christmas. She had taken a chance, a big one, and every day she worried that they would find out her secret.

As she finished the wreath, she turned and looked at the Christmas tree, twinkling with all of its multicolored lights. Even in her thirties, she had a glimmer of hope that one day she might get her life together enough to find a nice man, have children and start over again. But her life had been a series of false starts. Picking the wrong man. Making the wrong choices. Saying that next time she would do better.

The only problem was, she didn't know if she would ever have what she had always wanted. A person only got so many chances.

CHAPTER SEVEN

Meg was dead on her feet. Between work and school, and now Christmas carol practice a few nights this week, she just wanted to put on her flannel reindeer PJs and fall into a nice, warm bed. Instead, she was standing on the grass in the square singing Silent Night over and over because someone - probably her - couldn't stay in tune.

"Good Lord, one of you ladies is way off key!" Hen screeched again. Meg wanted to slowly walk backward and slink off into the night, but Hen would probably chase her down and tackle her. "Let's try this again."

They sang the song one more time, and Meg muted herself during the part that was causing issues. Thankfully, that seemed to appease Hen, and they were finally released for the night.

Christian was practicing some new fangled rendition of Jingle Bells with the other men from the group, but they finished right after the woman and dispersed too.

"I'm so tired," Meg said, falling into his arms. "Can we just go home and skip dinner?"

"You aren't hungry?"

"I am, but my stomach will understand," she said.

"Don't you think we should pick up Vivi from your mother?"

Meg's eyes opened wide. "What kind of mother am I? I totally forgot we need to pick up our child!"

Christian laughed. "You've been a little preoccupied, my love. It's okay."

As they walked toward the bookstore where Julie was working late, she held his hand. The beauty of the Christmas decorations on the square had her feeling the holiday spirit in a big way. She wanted to stop, drop to one knee and just propose to him herself. Change things up a bit. Surprise him. She stopped and looked up at him.

"Is something wrong?" he asked, looking at her with concern.

She couldn't form words. Drop to one knee, she thought to herself. Be brave.

"Meg?"

"Yeah?"

"Why did you stop? Are you okay?"

"I... um... Yes. I'm fine. I just thought my shoe was untied."

He looked down at her feet. "Darling, you're wearing flats."

She looked down too. "Oh."

Christian chuckled. "Boy, you do need a nice long sleep. Come on, let's get our daughter and go home."

* * *

SuAnn sat across from Nicholas and tried not to stare. As much as he resembled Santa Claus now, he was still as handsome as ever. The same blue-gray eyes she'd stared into thousands of times in high school. The same rough hands that loved to work in the yard and do his own mechanic work on his car. The same dimple in his left cheek, but not his right.

"Are you staring at me, Susie?" he said with a wink.

"Maybe a little. It's just so surreal that you're here."

Nick took a bite of chili and then wiped his mouth. They'd opted to have lunch at the cafe on the square before SuAnn was helping Julie with the cookie party later in the day.

"Well, I have to say it feels much the same for me. You're just as pretty as you ever were."

She smiled, trying desperately not to blush a bit, although her Irish heritage always gave her away.

"So what are we doing here?"

He tilted his head to the side in confusion. "I don't rightly know what you mean?"

"You and me. What are we doing?"

"We're eating lunch, honey. Are you feeling okay?"

She pursed her lips and squinted her eyes. "You know what I mean, Nicolas. Why are you here? What is it you think is going to happen with us? I mean, you don't live here. Are you just here to spend the holidays with an old flame?"

His eyes widened. "You're just as much of a spitfire now as you were back then. I'm here because I never stopped loving you."

"And I feel the same. You know that. But that was a

long time ago, and we were just kids. We're adults now, and we have to make mature decisions."

"What are you saying?"

"Look, I'm way too old to play games. And I'm somebody who appreciates reality. Logic. And I just don't see where we're going with this."

He folded his napkin and sat it in his empty bowl. "I've kind of been wanting to talk to you about that."

Here it comes, she thought. The big let down. No man in her life had ever not let her down at some point. She would rather just get it over with and enjoy her holidays than worry the whole time.

"Okay. What do you want to say?"

"I want you to move away with me."

SuAnn sat there, staring at him like she didn't understand the language she was speaking. "You want me to what?"

"Move away with me."

"What on earth are you talking about?"

He reached across the table and put his hand over hers. "Susie, we missed out on the chance to be together for decades. I want to make use of every bit of time we could have together. I don't know how you feel, but I don't ever want to be without you again."

"I feel the same way," she said, smiling.

"Then let's move away together. Let's go somewhere and have the life we always dreamed of. Remember when we said we would get a little place on the beach in Hawaii? Watch all of our sunsets together?"

"Those were the musings of two high school kids, Nick. We're grown up now."

"Why can't we have those dreams? Just me and you taking on the world!"

She rolled her eyes. "We're both in our seventies. I think our times of taking on the world are behind us, dear."

He laughed. "Maybe so, but can you imagine how much fun we would have? Or maybe we could check out Alaska? Or Montana? I've always wanted to move there. The fly fishing there is supposed to be amazing..."

She held up her hand. "Are you forgetting that I have a business here? And a life? My kids are here. My grandkids."

He leaned back in his chair a bit and nodded. "I know. I get that, I really do. I mean, I have nothing holding me anywhere because I never had kids, but I understand how difficult that must be for you."

She furrowed her eyebrows at him. "I don't think you can understand. Look, I had a rift with my daughters for so many years. It has taken us a lot of work over the last year to really get to a good place with each other, and picking up and leaving doesn't seem like the best move for me right now. Plus, I just opened my own business. I'm really proud of that."

He sighed. "Do you plan to spend the rest of your life living here because your family does? Do you want to work forever? I can take care of you, Susie. You'd never have to work again."

She felt so deflated. "This is the first time I've really had the life I wanted, Nick. I like it here. I have friends, and I really love running the bakery. It was a dream of mine for a long time."

"I don't remember you ever having that dream," he muttered.

"Well, I did. Not as a child, but as an adult. I spent my entire life being a wife and mother, and this is the first time I've had something for myself. I don't think I want to give that up."

"Not even for me?"

She sat there quietly. "I don't think it's fair for you to ask me to make such a huge decision when we've only been back together for a few days."

"I'm sorry. I don't mean to push. I just know I'm not getting any younger, Susie, and I'm ready to live the life I've always wanted."

She paused for a moment. "What happens if the life you want isn't the one I want?"

"I don't know. I guess that was a possibility I never considered."

* * *

Julie was so excited to have the Christmas cookie party. It was something she had done when her kids were little, and getting to watch her new son and her granddaughter experience the magic of Christmas was a blessing to her.

Dawson had been helping get everything ready, including buying cookie decorations at the store for her. She had so much to do lately that it felt like it was so hard to keep up. The one thing she didn't want to lose was the ability to experience the holidays. Sometimes people got so caught up in the holidays they didn't enjoy it. She was determined that would not happen to her.

"Is there anything else I can do?" Tina asked. She had been very helpful in the kitchen, getting things ready. Julie and Tina had made their own batch of sugar cookies even though people were going to be bringing plenty to decorate. The fire department was going to be overwhelmed with sweet treats by the end of the day.

"If you could put the tablecloth on the extra table. Since we're going to be decorating, I'd like to avoid having sprinkles all over the hardwood floors."

Even though it was the holidays, they didn't have anyone staying at the inn right now. Most people were with family, so they had cut off reservations until after the first of the year. It meant less money, but Julie was happy to have the place to themselves to enjoy the holidays as a family. Taking care of other people who were staying there took up a lot of time and energy, and right now she just wanted to focus on her family.

"No problem. Do you want the red tablecloth?"

Julie nodded. "Yes. And if you don't mind lighting a couple of those gingerbread candles in the foyer? They smell so good."

Tina nodded. "Will do. Just let me know if you need anything else."

Tina had been a big help with the Christmas festival and the preparations for the cookie party. She enjoyed having an extra helper, although she felt kind of bad asking her to do things since she technically was a guest.

"I'm here!" She heard her mother say as she walked through the front door. SuAnn looked at Tina, said nothing and kept walking. She didn't understand what problem her mother had with Tina, but she hoped she could behave herself today.

"Please tell me you brought the pound cakes?"

SuAnn rolled her eyes. "Of course I did. I even drizzled some red and green icing over the top of them. I'm sure the firefighters will love them. They often come into the bakery."

"I'm sure they will. Thanks. You can just put them over there on the counter."

Julie was running around like a chicken with its head cut off. Lots of people were going to be arriving any time now, and the house was going to be brimming with people talking, Christmas music playing and busy little hands making the cookies.

When her daughters had been young, this was one of her favorite memories. She hoped it would go off without a hitch and would become a new tradition for Dylan. He definitely needed traditions in his life. Traditions gave him roots.

"When is everybody going to be here?" Dylan asked, feverish with anticipation.

"Should be anytime now. I hope you have exercised your fingers and you're ready to decorate hundreds of cookies," she said, fixing the hair on top of his head.

"I'm ready!" he said, running off into the living room. He spent most of his time sitting beside the Christmas tree, trying to keep himself from shaking the presents that Julie had already placed under it. Most of his things hadn't been wrapped yet and were hidden up in the attic, but he didn't need to know that.

Dawson, trying to be sly, had her put pennies in several of the gifts just so that when he shook them, he had no idea what was inside. It was a cruel little trick that Dawson said they had done in his family for years.

"Anybody home?" Janine said as she came through the front door with William following behind her.

Shortly after, Colleen and Tucker walked into the kitchen.

"Where do you want us to put these cookies?" Colleen asked.

"On the counter, please."

Over the next few minutes, everybody arrived, stacks of cookies in all different colored plastic containers lined the kitchen counters. Dawson put out all the different colored sprinkles, chocolate chips, and everything else he had bought for decorations.

Janine had bought pre-made sugar cookies from the grocery store, probably knowing her limits as a cook. She was the only person Julie thought could burn water.

Colleen had made different cookie shapes, including candy canes and gingerbread men. They looked a little brown around the edges, but Julie wasn't about to tell her that.

When Dixie arrived, she had an arm full of fruit cakes, and Carrie was carrying a bowl of sugar cookies she had made. Harry wasn't there, opting to stay out of the frenzy.

Julie noticed her mother standing off to the side, not saying much. That wasn't normal for SuAnn, and she wondered where Nick was. She had assumed that he would come.

"Are you okay?"

"Of course. Why wouldn't I be?"

"You just seem a little... down."

SuAnn shrugged her shoulders. "Probably just tired. I've been pretty busy at the bakery."

"Where's Nick? I thought he was coming?"

"We had lunch earlier. We decided that it was best

for him to run a few errands instead of coming today."
She wasn't making eye contact, which was a sure sign
that something was going on. Julie decided not to pick
at that string since the cookie party was in full swing
and she definitely didn't want to create any drama.

"Hey, do you mind helping Dylan wash his hands?
Sometimes when I ask him to do that, he just quickly
runs them under the water with no soap. I don't want
him making cookies for the firefighters with dirty little
hands."

SuAnn nodded her head. "Of course. I'll take him
upstairs."

She watched as her mother went and corralled
Dylan, ushering him toward the stairs. She definitely
looked upset, almost sad. Julie wondered if something
had happened between her and Nick, and maybe he'd
already left town. She hoped not. Their high school love
story was something that made Julie smile, and she
wanted her mother to have a new chance at love.

"You alright?" Dawson asked, walking up behind her
and squeezing her shoulders.

"Yes, but I think something's going on with my
mother and Nick, but I can't worry about it right now."

He turned her around, putting his hands on both of
her cheeks. "This day is for you and Dylan. This is your
chance to make a new memory with your son, so don't
worry about your mother right now. Her love life can
wait."

"I know you're right. I just always want everybody to
have a perfect Christmas."

"I only care about my wife and son having a perfect
Christmas. Everybody else is just going to have to figure

it out for themselves," Dawson said, smiling at her and then kissing her forehead.

"Break it up," Meg said as she walked into the kitchen with Vivi on her hip. "Nobody wants to see that public display of affection."

Dawson laughed. "Well, you're not going to like this then." He dipped Julie backward and planted a kiss on her lips. Meg groaned.

"You old people are gross sometimes."

"They are gross all the time!" Dylan chimed in as he ran back into the kitchen. "Every morning they're kissing each other. Sometimes it makes me nauseous when I'm eating my pancakes!"

Julie and Dawson laughed. "Good, then we're doing something right!" Julie said.

"When are we going to decorate the cookies?"

"We're going to start right now. Come on. I'll show you what to do."

* * *

Colleen and Tucker sat at the table with her mother, Dawson and Dylan. She couldn't even count how many cookies were on the table. Sprinkles were everywhere, and Julie had given up trying to pick them up off the floor. She said the robotic vacuum would figure it out later.

"Look at this one!" Dylan said, holding up the gingerbread cookie he had decorated. "I think this is my best one!" So far, he'd thought every one he decorated was the best one.

"It looks great," Colleen said, smiling at her new little brother. She had to admit, having a little brother was something she had never imagined for herself, especially at her age. But now she did, and she loved him with her whole heart.

"Can I keep this one instead of taking it to the firefighters?"

Julie smiled. "I suppose so, but you've kept about ten of them. Where are you putting them, anyway?"

"On the bookshelf over there," Dylan said, pointing across the room to Dawson's grandmother's antique bookshelf.

Julie's eyes widened. "Dylan, how about taking them into the kitchen? Put them on a plate and hide them in the laundry room."

"Yes ma'am," he said, groaning. He walked over to the bookcase and collected his hidden cookies before disappearing into the kitchen.

"That kid has more energy than ten wild animals put together," Dawson said, shaking his head.

"He cracks me up," Colleen said. "But watching you raise a nine-year-old is even more hysterical. I never thought I would see the day that I'd have a little brother."

"Well, I never thought I'd have a son," Julie said. She continued icing the cookie in front of her. "But he's been a wonderful blessing for us. I just can't wait to see what he does in the future."

"I can promise you it will be something that requires a lot of energy," Dawson said, taking a bite out of his cookie.

Julie slapped him on the arm. "You're supposed to be a good example! What are you doing eating the cookies?"

He stared at her for a moment. "Julie, honey, we

have like three-thousand cookies here. There's a hundred people sitting in our living room decorating them right now. The firefighters will not go hungry if I eat a couple of cookies."

"I think you are overestimating the number of cookies or people here. Stop eating them! We want to give them all to the fire station."

"Are you telling me we're not going to keep any of these cookies for ourselves?"

"We'll keep a few. But you're going to be so big you're going to need to borrow William's Santa Claus costume."

Tucker laughed. "Is this what being married is like?"

Colleen elbowed him. "Do you have a problem with that?"

"No, dear," he said, hanging his head like he was a dominated husband before chuckling under his breath.

"So, I hear congratulations are in order about a new toy line you might work on next Christmas?" Dawson said.

"Yeah. It's a really exciting opportunity with Jamison O'Malley's company. I thought it would take me years to accomplish something like that."

"That's great, Tucker. I know you've worked really hard for this," Julie said, picking up another plain cookie and beginning the decorating process again.

"We wanted to talk to you guys about something," Colleen said, looking at Tucker nervously.

"Okay. What's going on?" Julie asked, putting the cookie back down on the table.

"Well... There's been a pretty major change in our lives."

"Did you get engaged?"

"No, Mom. Don't you think I would've told you that?"

"Besides, I'm terrified to ask her again. She broke my heart into pieces the last time," Tucker said, putting his hand over his chest dramatically.

"You're not funny," Colleen whispered.

"What's this big change?" Julie asked getting impatient.

"We spoke to Jamison O'Malley yesterday, and in order for this opportunity to come to fruition, he's going to need us to come to New York City for a few months after the first of the year."

Julie's face fell a bit. "A few months?"

"Yes. He wants us to work right there in his offices in Manhattan. Really work closely with his team in a way that he doesn't think we can do remotely."

"But, I'll miss you. I'm used to having both of my girls here in Seagrove."

Colleen reached across the table and squeezed her mother's hand. "I know. And we will miss this place too. Trust me, we're not planning on staying in New York City for any longer than we have to. We will be right back in Seagrove as soon as possible."

"Congratulations, you two. What an honor to be invited to do something like this, and I'm sure it's going to be a financial success for you," Dawson said, putting his arm around Julie as if he was trying to pull her into the same way of thinking.

"I hope you're happy for us, Mom?" Colleen said.

Julie smiled. "I am extremely happy for both of you.

And so proud. I'm sad for me, but thrilled for you. At least we can video chat every day!"

"Yes, technology is a wonderful thing," Tucker said. "And don't worry, Julie, I promise I'll take good care of your daughter."

Julie smiled at him. "I have no doubt about that, Tucker."

CHAPTER EIGHT

*O*ne of the people that Julie was so happy that she had invited to the cookie party was Amy, the social worker who had first helped to set up the camp that led to them finding Dylan. She thought it was a perfect way to thank her and include her in their holiday festivities. Plus, Dylan was really excited to see her again.

"I'm so happy that you could come! I know everything is really busy around the holiday season," Julie said, giving her a hug.

Amy smiled. "I wouldn't miss this for the world. Dylan was always one of my favorites, and it's been months since I've seen him. I know that he is doing so well with you guys, and he's happier than I've ever seen him. Just look at that grin on his face!" She pointed across the room where Dylan was sitting at a table with Meg and Christian decorating his cookies. He had made the rounds already, going from table to table showing off his cookie decorating skills.

"I never thought I'd be a mother again at this age, but it has been delightful. He's a handful, don't get me wrong. One of the most energetic kids I think I've ever met, but he's so smart and sweet and talented."

"Of course, Julie isn't just slightly biased," Dawson said.

As they were speaking, Tina walked by, carrying another tray of plain cookies to one of the tables.

"Tina, come here. I'd like you to meet someone," Julie said. For a moment, Tina looked a little hesitant, probably because she wasn't very good at meeting new people. In fact, she was one of the shyest people that Julie had ever met.

"Hi," Tina said, barely looking up at Amy.

Amy eyed her carefully. "Hi. I'm Amy, the social worker that put Dylan with Julie and Dawson. And you are?"

"Tina. I am just staying here during the holidays," she said, stuttering over her words.

"You look so familiar. Have we met before?"

Tina shook her head no. "I don't think so. I'm not really from around here. I was just coming to see some family."

"Maybe I know your family. Who are you visiting?"

"Um... my cousins... You probably wouldn't know them. They don't actually live right here in Seagrove..."

Julie couldn't understand why Tina seemed so incredibly uncomfortable. But she felt bad for putting her in that situation and wanted to do whatever she needed to get her out of it.

"Oh, Tina, can you go check with Lucy and see if she'll make a new pot of coffee?"

Tina, seeming thrilled to get out of the situation, quickly disappeared back into the kitchen.

"She's very shy. She didn't really have anyone to spend the holidays with and I think she just made up a story about her family, honestly. She has a very sad history, but she doesn't talk a lot about it."

Amy stared at the kitchen door for a moment and then looked back at Julie. "It's uncanny. She must look like somebody I know. But anyway, I'm glad you're helping her at the holidays. Nobody should be alone at Christmas time."

Julie thought the same thing. If at no other time of the year, people shouldn't be alone at Christmas.

* * *

SuAnn sat across from Dixie, the few cookies she had decorated sitting in front of her. She knew she should work faster, especially since she worked in the bakery every day. This should've been exactly what she was good at. But, right now, she just felt like the wind had been let out of her sails.

"Honey, are you okay?" Dixie asked, that deep southern twang of hers enveloping every word like a warm sweater.

"I'm fine. Why do you ask?" SuAnn said, staring down at her cookies and speaking in a monotone voice.

"Oh Lord, it must be man trouble. I hear you had an old flame come back and find you?"

"I swear, small towns are rumor mills," SuAnn muttered.

"Well, it ain't a rumor if it's true," Dixie said, smearing red icing on a candy cane cookie. Carrie had walked into the kitchen to help Julie package up some of the cookies for the firefighters.

"I wish everybody would just stay out of my business."

"No, you don't."

"Excuse me?"

"If you wanted everybody to stay out of your business, then you'd put a smile on that scowling face of yours. But you're not doing that because you're upset about something, and you want people to know it."

"Dixie, just decorate your cookies," she said, exasperated.

"Look, the way I see it is we're both in our golden years, so you should be able to confide in me about this sort of thing. None of these young women are going to understand."

"Since when are we best friends?"

"Do you want me to call Hen?"

"No. Hen is busy with the Christmas festival. And besides, I'm not asking for counseling about anything. And you're getting that red icing all over the tablecloth," SuAnn said, pointing at the cookie that Dixie wasn't paying close enough attention to.

"Well, excuse me. I do have Parkinson's disease and shake a bit. Be happy I'm not flinging this icing all over the room. The marvels of modern medicine are keeping this hand pretty steady," Dixie said with a laugh. "The other night, you should've seen me and Harry trying to put cinnamon on our sweet potatoes. Poor Carrie had to clean up our mess!"

"I've never seen anybody make fun of such a serious medical diagnosis.

"Honey, if I don't make fun of things, I'd be sitting in the corner crying all the time. And I have a life to live! I don't have time to be sitting around sulking and worrying about the future. All I have is today, and I'm going to make it the best day I can."

SuAnn sat there for a minute, contemplating whether she should confide in Dixie. After all, if anybody was going to understand her predicament, it would be Dixie.

"Nick and I had a little argument earlier today."

"What kind of argument?"

SuAnn pushed her cookies aside and leaned on her forearms. "The kind that could mean the end of our relationship before it even starts."

"You two were high school sweethearts. What on earth could you be arguing about already?"

"He wants me to run away with him. Move to Hawaii or Montana or something. I tried to explain to him I just got my life going here. I have my business and my girls. I don't want to take off and live somewhere else where I don't know anybody."

"And he does?"

"Very much so. He said it's his big dream. And I just said that maybe we don't have the same dreams. Honestly, I kind of wish he never came to town because he gave me a taste of what I've been missing in my life and now he might go somewhere else."

"Well, that is a dilemma. My Harry was okay staying here but doing some traveling in the RV. Maybe you could suggest that to him?"

SuAnn shook her head. "I don't think so. If he really

cared about me, he would've listened to what I was saying. He would care about what I care about."

"Well, pardon me for asking this, but do you care about what he cares about?"

"What do you mean?"

"Well, it seems to me that you're only thinking about yourself here, SuAnn."

"What a horrible thing to say!"

"I didn't mean to sound ugly. I just mean that you want him to care about your hopes and dreams. Have you thought about asking him about his?"

"He already told me! He wants to run away and act like a couple of teenagers in love."

"It sounds to me like he wants some adventure in his life. Some excitement. And he's been waiting for you all these years. Doesn't that tell you something?"

"It tells me he's immature and thinks he can just waltz around the world for the rest of his days."

"You know, it's not so bad to have a healthy, energetic, mature man. Maybe you need a little more excitement in your life?"

"I get plenty of excitement here."

Dixie laughed so loudly that people turned around at the other tables. "I love Seagrove. You know that. But there ain't a lot of excitement going on around here."

"I think excitement is overrated anyway," SuAnn said, picking up another cookie and angrily starting to slather icing on it. "Buddy and I did plenty of traveling, and it sure didn't help us stay married."

"Because you didn't love him, and you know it. You

were bored. Maybe you're just scared to step out there and do something new?"

"You would've made a terrible psychologist," SuAnn said, knowing full well that Dixie might have a point.

"Well, that's a good thing because I was never planning on becoming a psychologist. But I am an old woman, so I have old woman wisdom. And I'm telling you, you don't need to let this guy go. He's pined for you his entire life, so you need to do your part to see if you can make it work out."

"And if I can't?"

Dixie shrugged her shoulders. "Then you know you tried. And you can go on with your life with no regrets."

She had a point there. Maybe all she could do at this point was to have a heart to heart talk with Nick and just see if they were compatible anymore. A part of her was terrified that they weren't.

* * *

"Okay, everybody, we have all of the cookies packaged up. We're gonna need everybody to help carry some of them out to Dawson's truck. Then we will just pile into as many vehicles as we need to and head on over to the fire station."

"What are we doing when we get there?" Dylan asked.

Julie smiled at him, knowing full well that she had explained this at least five times over the previous few days. Sometimes she didn't think he listened with his ears at all. "We're going to drive over there and we're going to thank the firefighters for serving the community all throughout the year. We will carry these cookies into their kitchen, along with the pound cake and fruit cakes. And, if they're not busy, they may give us a really nice tour of the fire station."

"Will, I get to sit in the fire truck?" Dylan asked, excitedly.

"Maybe so. One year, they even pulled the firetruck out and raised up the really tall ladder with a bucket on the end. My girls got to stand in it high up in the air with one of the firemen."

"I hope they do that!" Dylan said, clapping his hands.

"Don't count on it. Things were a lot different back then," Dawson said. He leaned over and whispered into Julie's ear. "Back before people would sue anybody for anything."

She laughed. "All right, everybody out the door. Grab some cookies!"

For the next few minutes, there was a flurry of activity in the kitchen as each person grabbed what they could and walked out to Dawson's truck. They carefully packed it all up so it wouldn't fly around in the bed of the truck on the way to the fire station.

When they finally had everything packaged, Julie and Dylan climbed into Dawson's truck along with SuAnn, who was catching a ride with them. She had been silent most of the afternoon, except when Julie saw her sitting at the table talking to Dixie. She could only hope that Dixie was setting her straight on whatever was going on.

"Are they following us?" Julie asked, looking out the side mirror.

Dawson reached over and squeezed her leg. "Stop stressing out, Julie. Everybody knows where the fire station is. I doubt they're going to get lost on the way."

She laughed because she knew he was right. She was stressing over every little detail today. Her perfectionistic tendencies were coming out, what with her involvement in the Christmas festival too. She wanted everything to go smoothly, but she knew she had a high likelihood of crashing as soon as the holidays were over.

"Can you turn some air on? I'm having a heat stroke back here," SuAnn said.

"Mother, it's December. Why on earth would you need air conditioning?"

"I don't know, Julie. I guess it's because I'm at a certain stage of life, and I'd like to have a little cold air blowing on me. Do you have to make everything such a big deal? Plus, we're in the lowcountry, not Alaska! It's still warm here."

Yes, there was definitely something going on with her mother. Although SuAnn had a tendency to speak her mind, she was definitely on edge today more than normal.

"Fine. I'll roll down your window a little."

"Well, you're gonna mess up my hair, but whatever" she heard her mother mutter under her breath.

She cracked SuAnn's window and then looked over at Dawson. He gave her a look as if to say just ignore it. Ignoring her mother was difficult, as it was for many daughters. That relationship between mother and daughter could be treacherous.

A few minutes later, they pulled into the fire station. An older red brick building, the fire station has been in the same place for many years, according to Dawson.

He thought they might renovate it one day, but it didn't seem to be high on the list of the city council's concerns.

"Do they have a pole in here that the firefighters slide down?" Dylan asked as they parked the truck.

"I don't know. We'll have to ask one of the firemen," Dawson said.

"Do they have fire ladies?" Dylan asked.

"I'm sure they do. Now, stop with the questions for a little while and save some for the firefighters," Julie said, exhausted from answering the thousand questions he had asked just in that one day. She forgot how inquisitive little kids were.

Once on a trip to Kentucky to see some distant relatives, Meg had decided not to go to sleep and had asked what seemed to be four-thousand questions on the way there. By the time they got to Kentucky, Julie had been ready to pull her hair out by the roots.

"I'll get the cookies!" Dylan said, jumping out of the truck as quickly as he could. Dawson was already back there, waiting for everybody to park and handing out cookies to those who were standing there.

As Julie watched the process happen, she was so thankful to get to create this new memory with Dylan and Vivi. Although Vivi was so little she probably wouldn't remember this first part. But they planned to do it every year, and she would make sure it was a part of her granddaughter's life.

Giving back to the community and saying thank you to first responders was an important part of how she had raised her own daughters, and she hoped to raise her new son the same way. She wanted him to be thankful for those who served the community, and to at least show thanks at the holiday season.

   * * *

The firefighters had been thrilled to receive all the cookies and cakes. Of course, as Julie expected, there were tons of treats already in the kitchen brought by people in the community. But she still liked to do it, if for nothing else than to just show her appreciation.

Dylan was very excited about the tour. As they walked through in a large group, the firefighters showed them all the different areas, including their living room where they played games and watched TV when they weren't on calls. They also showed their kitchen where they prepared meals. One of the firemen had explained that he was the main cook of the group, and some of them were terrible in the kitchen.

They walked out into the sleeping quarters, and Dylan seemed to be very surprised by them. They were more like cubicles with little beds in them, and he couldn't imagine that the firefighters slept in those rooms with no actual walls or privacy.

"What happens when you need to use the bathroom?" Dylan suddenly blurted out. Julie wanted to slip her hand around his mouth, but it was too late.

"Well, we use the bathroom," the firefighter said. His name was Steve, and he was a tall, muscular guy with bright red hair and broad shoulders. Julie could imagine him carrying just about anyone out of a burning building without an issue.

"But does the bathroom have a door? Or does it look like this where you all use the bathroom in the same room?"

Julie didn't know where Dylan got these questions. She was so embarrassed, but couldn't help but laugh.

Steve smiled. "It's a private bathroom. Don't worry."

They continued walking around the place until they ended up in the large bay where there was one firetruck and an ambulance.

"As you can see, this is our main fire truck. We have another one that's out on a call helping out with a fire in Charleston. And then this is our ambulance. We don't get a lot of emergency calls around here except for the occasional chest pain or fender bender. "

"What's a fender bender?" Dylan called out.

"Usually it's just a minor accident between a couple of cars."

"Oh. Boring."

"Dylan, would you like to climb into the firetruck and see all the different buttons?"

Dylan grinned from ear to ear. "Yes! I think I might want to be a firefighter when I grow up."

"Hey! I thought you wanted to be a carpenter?" Dawson said, laughing.

"I want to be a carpenter and a firefighter," Dylan responded before running over to the fire truck.

Steve put a fire hat on him and helped him climb up into the truck.

"That kid. Where does he come up with these crazy questions?" Dawson said.

"Oh, my William here used to ask some doozies," Dixie said, pointing to her son. "I remember one time..."

William walked over and hugged his mother from

behind. "Let's not tell stories right now, Mom. They never end well for me."

She giggled. "Okay, just know I remember all of them and I'm ready to pull them out at a moment's notice."

Julie watched as Dylan walked all the way around the fire truck as Steve told him all sorts of different things about it. His eyes were wide, and of course he was asking tons of questions.

When they were done, everybody stood in a group in front of several firefighters who had been there working the whole time. Julie loved Dawson, but she had to admit most firefighters were handsome. She hadn't seen an ugly one yet.

"Thank you all so much for making the cookies for us," Steve said.

"You're very welcome. And thank you for serving the community. We don't do enough to show our gratitude, but just know that we are very thankful for all that you do," Julie said.

After saying their goodbyes, everybody loaded back up into their cars. Dylan was a bit quieter than expected as they drove down the road back toward the inn.

"What's the matter? I thought you'd be all smiles after that visit," Julie said, looking at him.

"That was a lot of fun, But I'm a little sad about something."

"What's that?"

"I'm not going to be able to be a firefighter for a lot of years. All I get to be is just a stupid kid."

"Don't worry. Adulthood will come soon enough,

Dylan. And you'll wish you were a kid again," Dawson said, laughing.

* * *

When Julie opened her eyes the next morning, she couldn't believe it was the day of the festival. After so much preparation, it was finally time to celebrate with the entire town. She would be glad when it was over so she could completely focus on Christmas morning. In fact, she still had a ton of Christmas shopping to do because Dylan's list seemed to get longer and longer. She knew she shouldn't be buying everything he wanted, not wanting to spoil him, but she just couldn't help herself.

"Good morning," Dawson said, sitting on the edge of the bed. He had been up for a while, probably working on his super secret project in the barn. It had been all she could do not to go in there and try to figure out what he was working on, but she didn't want to ruin the surprise for him or for herself.

"Good morning," she said. He handed her a cup of coffee, something he often did when he woke up before her.

"How'd you sleep?"

"After that party, I slept really well. I'm surprised the sugar from eating all the broken cookies didn't keep me up all night."

"I'm surprised Dylan wasn't bouncing off the walls."

Julie laughed. "No, he was down for the count last night. He went to sleep and that was that. Maybe we should make him do more things during the day to get sleepy." She sat up in the bed and took a sip of her coffee.

"I was going to head into town to help set up for the festival this evening. Do you need me to do anything before I go?"

"Well, if you could load up a bunch of those wreaths, that would be helpful. Otherwise, me and Tina are going to have to load them into my car, and I don't think they'll all fit."

"No problem. I'll get them there. Anything else?"

"Nope. I guess I'll see you this afternoon when I head over. I don't want to miss the caroling since Meg and Christian are doing it."

"Oh, that's right. I guess we'll have Vivi?"

"No, I think Colleen is going to keep her."

"Okay then. Remember, don't go snooping around the barn," he said as he stood up and quickly kissed her on the head.

"I won't," she called, still fighting off the urge to just peek into the one of the windows.

As she watched her husband walk out the door, she felt an overwhelming sense of gratitude for the gift of their marriage. When Michael had destroyed their relationship, she'd been at her lowest, thinking second chances didn't happen for most people. Now, here she was living a life she could've never dreamed of because it was so beyond anything she would have imagined for herself. It just went to show that sometimes God's plans were so much bigger than a human's brain could even comprehend.

CHAPTER NINE

SuAnn's favorite time of the day had always been morning. She loved getting to the bakery early and beginning her work to create the best pound cakes the town had ever known.

Still, her heart was heavy this morning after the discussion that she had with Nick. She had no idea where they stood, and that was making her feel very uneasy. In fact, she hadn't talked to him since the day before, and she worried that he had already left town. Maybe he decided being with her wasn't worth it, after all.

"Good morning," Darcy said as she walked through the back door.

"Good morning. If you don't mind cutting up the cakes I set aside for the festival, that would be great. We're going to be handing out samples."

"No problem. How was the cookie party yesterday?"

SuAnn stirred the ingredients for her favorite gingerbread pound cake in a large stainless steel bowl.

"It was fun. My new grandson had a great time at the fire station tour."

Darcy nodded. "You seem a little down today. Is everything okay?"

"Oh, it's fine. Just pesky life stuff."

Darcy reached for the large serrated bread knife and put one of the pound cakes on the cutting board in front of her. "It sounds more like it might be relationship stuff?"

"I don't have a relationship," SuAnn said, continuing to stir.

"I thought things were going pretty well with you and that Nick fellow that came searching for you?"

"So did I."

Just as she was sure that Darcy was going to stick her nose into her business, the door opened, the loud bell announcing the arrival of a customer. SuAnn took that as an opportunity to go into the back room and let Darcy take the lead. She could hear her out there, chatting up their regular customers, ringing up their orders and pouring their coffee. This morning, she just didn't feel like doing any of it.

This was the perk of owning her own business. She could decide on when she worked, how late she worked, and what she did when she got to work. But she would leave each day feeling proud of her accomplishments.

For most of her life, she had been a caretaker. Being a mother and a wife for so many years, she never had a lot of time for herself. All of her dreams had gotten pushed to the back burner a long time ago. That was why the bakery meant so much to her.

It was the first thing she had built from the ground

up, all by herself. Its success or failure depended completely on her. All the responsibilities rested on her shoulders, and she liked that. If she was honest with herself, she wanted other people to admire her accomplishments because that had never happened before.

Although she had loved being a mother, this was a time in her life that she felt belonged to her. She wanted to see what she could accomplish, and that's why Nick wanting her to leave Seagrove when she had just gotten started with her business made her feel so upset. It was like she was having to choose between the two great dreams of her life - owning a successful business and having a relationship with the person she believed to be her soulmate.

"Darcy?"

"Yeah?" Darcy said, after finishing up with the last customer that had come during the morning rush.

"I know it's highly irregular for me to do this, but do you mind if I leave you here alone for a little while? I just want to take a walk and clear my head."

"Of course. You're the boss anyway," she said in her normal blunt style.

"Very true," SuAnn said, reaching for her cardigan sweater on the hook where she hung it next to her apron. "I'll be back soon."

As she walked out onto the town square, she looked around at her new hometown. Never had she thought this place would have grown on her so quickly, but it did. The people were friendly and they accepted her for who she was. The scenery was beautiful. And, best of all, her family was there.

She loved how the town had decorated the square

for the holidays. They had wrapped each of the quaint light posts in garland and lights. On the light poles, they had also attached lit up candy canes with silver and red tinsel attached.

In the center of the square, where the grassy area was, there was a nativity scene, temporary ice-skating rink and of course the Christmas tree that would be lit later that night.

Sometimes she looked around Seagrove and thought about how it was like a town out of some past era that didn't exist anywhere else anymore. It often reminded her of her own childhood when things were simpler and she could go to the corner drugstore and get a soda.

Maybe that was why she had fallen in love with the town because it reminded her so much of her younger years. Maybe simple was exactly what she wanted in her life, and that was why traveling to some remote place with Nick wasn't appealing.

"Are you lost?"

She turned to see Nick leaning against one of the light posts. It reminded her of how he looked back in high school when he would lean against the wall outside of her math class waiting to walk her to science. He'd been so handsome then, with a thick mane of dark brown hair and broad shoulders. Somehow, he was even more handsome now. A long life and plenty of earned wisdom had served him well.

"Are you accusing me of having dementia?"

He chuckled. "No. Just trying to sound funny. I can see I didn't hit the mark."

She kept walking, albeit at a slower pace since she was hoping he would try to keep up. He fell in step behind her, eventually meeting her stride. She continued staring straight ahead, but having no particular place she was going. Her intention was just to walk round and round the square.

"Are you not speaking to me?"

"I never said that."

"But it seems that way."

"Look, I'm not the one who decided he wants to gallivant around the world. I'm perfectly happy right where I am, so it seems we are at cross purposes here."

"Susie, I don't want to bash the wonderful business you've built for yourself. That's not what I meant to do at all. You should know better than anybody that I sometimes stick my foot in my mouth."

She chuckled under her breath. "Yes, I do remember that about you."

"And if I remember correctly, you do that your fair share too."

"I won't admit to that."

"It's just that I've dreamed my entire life that we would find our way back to each other, and I want to give you the world."

She stopped and looked at him. "I don't want the world. What if I want you and my business and my kids?"

"That just seems like such a letdown."

"Excuse me? A letdown?" she said, putting her hand on her hip.

"See? I just stuck my foot in my mouth again. I meant a letdown for you."

"Why would it be a letdown for me?"

"I know that you've been a wife and mother for

most of your life. And now you have all of this freedom, and I feel like I need to show you the world that you haven't seen yet. Take you places. Have adventures with you we didn't get to have when we were younger."

"But what if everything I want is here, including you? What if I don't want to do all that traveling? Are you going to be okay living the simple life right here in Seagrove?"

"Susie," he said, putting his hands on her upper arms. "I have the rest of my life planned out. And the only thing written on that list is to be near you. So, if this is where you want to be, then this is where I'll be. But I still want to go fishing in Montana at some point."

She couldn't help but laugh out loud. "How about this? Twice a year, we plan some amazing trip, and I leave my bakery in the hands of my capable assistant, Darcy."

Nick grinned. "I do believe that sounds like the perfect plan. So, I guess I better look for a house for me right here in Seagrove. Looks like I'll be staying a while."

She looked up at him. "With any luck, you'll be staying here with me forever."

"That sounds like a dream come true, Susie Q."

They walked arm in arm down the sidewalk, and SuAnn couldn't believe her good fortune. Maybe she was going to have her own second chance after all.

* * *

"But where is he?" Julie asked, holding the phone to her ear. How could a Christmas festival be this incredibly stressful? "The kids are already lining up... I understand that he's not feeling well but..."

She paced back-and-forth on the grass right in front of the nativity scene. For some reason, she felt very exposed right in front of baby Jesus. She didn't want to say anything inappropriate, but she was getting pretty irate.

The man they had hired to play Santa Claus for the children's pictures had called out sick an hour before he was set to start the job. He had been Santa Claus at the Christmas festival for the last six years, but he had to pick this day to come down with the flu.

"I understand. Thank you for letting me know and please tell Wendall that we hope he feels better soon." Right now, she honestly wanted to throttle Wendell, but it didn't seem in keeping with the Christmas spirit to say that out loud.

As she pressed end on the call, she couldn't help but freak out a little. There was already a line of kids and parents forming in front of the Santa Claus display, and the only person there was an elf who looked very lonely. She didn't know what they were going to do.

"Janine!" she called from across the grassy area. Janine was helping to set up the cakewalk game that they would play later in the evening.

"What's up?" she asked, breathless from running across the square.

"We have a major problem. Santa Claus has the flu."

"Oh no, I hope Rudolph doesn't catch it!" Janine said, laughing.

"This is no time for joking. Kids are lined up already, and there's not going to be a Santa Claus."

"Well, what are we going to do?"

"Do you think William would..."

"Absolutely not. William vowed never to put that costume on again. He's glad to give it to someone else, but he's not the jolliest Santa Claus I've ever seen."

"I don't know what to do..." Julie looked around at all the people. "Wait. I have an idea."

She ran off in the other direction with Janine watching her in confusion. She had seen her mom and Nick walking around the square, arm in arm and obviously not having problems anymore. Now was the time to strike if she needed a favor.

"Mom!" she said, running up behind them.

"Julie? Dear, you are really messing up your hair by running around like this. Do you want to be sweaty in front of all the people in town?"

Julie rolled her eyes. "Please. Not now. You must be Nick?"

"Yes, I am. It's very nice to meet you, Julie."

Julie smiled. "Nice to meet you too. Listen, I'm in a bind so I'm going to cut right to the chase. I can't help but notice how much you look like Santa Claus."

"Julie! Honestly, remember your manners!"

"It's okay, Susie. Everybody says that."

"I'm sorry. I didn't mean to be rude, but I'm kind of in a time crunch here and our Santa Claus just called out sick with the flu. I have a line of kids over there ready to sit on Santa's lap and get their picture taken."

Nick chuckled. "And you'd like for me to put on a red suit and sit in that chair, right?"

She put her hands in the prayer position. "Please? You'll save the Christmas festival if you do this."

"No problem. I've played Santa Claus my fair share

of times in my life. Susie, would you like to be Mrs. Claus?"

SuAnn shook her head. "I think I'll give you a no on that one. Besides, I have to get back and help Darcy at the store. We'll be closing early today to take part in the festival, and I've left her there alone for a couple of hours already."

Nick leaned in and gave her a quick kiss on the cheek. "I'll see you in a little while." As Julie walked away with Nick, she saw him look back one more time at her mother.

"You two are very cute."

He chuckled. "I have to tell you, I can't remember a time in my life that I've been so happy to see somebody again. Your mom is just like I remembered her."

Julie had to giggle inside about that. There weren't many men in the world who could handle her mother, so if this one loved her just how she was, he was good in her book.

* * *

"So explain to me again how this works? They just walk in a circle and then the music stops? Like musical chairs?" William asked.

"Kind of. Except when the music stops, we don't kick that person out of the game. We draw a number from this hat and we call it out. Whoever is standing on that number gets to pick one cake as a prize."

He nodded. " And people enjoy this?"

Janine elbowed him. "Yes, they do. Don't be a sourpuss."

"I'm just really looking forward to the tree lighting later tonight."

"Oh yeah? Why is that?"

"I don't know. I guess it brings back memories from when I was a kid. I used to love watching them light the tree. Back in those days, we did it just after Thanksgiving, but I guess it's okay that we do it at the Christmas festival now. When I was a kid, my dad would hoist me up on his shoulders so I could get the best view in town."

"That's a sweet memory."

"It is. He always made holidays special. Not that my mom doesn't. I guess I'm just missing my dad lately."

"Your dad would be so proud of the man you've become, William. I have no doubt about that."

"Thanks."

"I guess I need to get a tree for the yoga studio soon. Maybe you could help me pick one out?"

"Of course. Now that the boat parade is behind us, I've got plenty of time on my hands," he said with a laugh.

"Did you meet Mom's boyfriend?" Julie asked as she walked up, frazzled as usual.

"I did. He's the perfect Santa Claus! He seems like a really nice guy."

"He basically told me that Mom is his dream woman. Can you imagine that?" Julie said, giggling.

"They say there's a lid for every pot," William said. The women looked at him. "What? My mom says that all the time."

"Still, it's funny to hear it come out of your mouth," Janine said, laughing.

"What's so funny?" Dixie asked as she walked up with Harry following closely behind her.

"Your son is turning into you," Janine said, putting her arm around his waist.

Dixie reached up and pinched his cheek. "Good! I happen to think I'm wonderful!"

"And modest." William said, rolling his eyes.

"So, how can we help?"

"Well, if you and Harry don't mind doing a little organizing of the cakes over on the table, that would be great. And William and I are going to start putting the numbers on the ground," Janine said.

Dixie did as she was told and started re-organizing the cakes and pies that were lining the long folding tables on the edge of the grassy area.

Janine looked around at all the families enjoying the festival so far. Things hadn't even gotten into full swing yet, and they would certainly get more festive when the sun went down. It was good to see so many cheerful people, laughing and smiling, and children running all over the place.

Off in the distance, she could see Nick playing the part of Santa Claus, each little kid sitting on his lap and whispering in his ear what they wanted for Christmas. The photographer was steadily taking photos, and parents were happily paying to get their prints at the other end of the line. The money would go into the town coffers, probably to fix up some roads or buy school supplies.

The great thing about Seagrove was that everybody did their part. People were so nice here that it was sometimes hard to believe, and Janine had traveled all over the world. To find a place like this to call home was special, which was why she never planned to leave.

* * *

Meg stood there, going over the words in her mind. It wasn't like she was going to be singing a solo or anything, but she certainly didn't want to be the person to yell out the wrong word during any of her songs.

Christian, with his thick French accent, sounded like he should be a singer on the radio. She sounded like she should sing down in the sewers.

"We go on in just a few minutes," Christian said as he walked over. The men and women would sing separately and then coming together for a couple of songs at the end. The school had donated a platform from the chorus department for them to stand on. She felt like she was about to be on full display, which was something she had never overly enjoyed.

"I'll be so glad when this is over," she said, nervously rubbing her hands together. He took both of her hands and squeezed them.

"This is going to be a very special night, Meg."

"Do you think so? Because I'm just thinking about all the things that could go wrong."

"Have fun! It's just Christmas caroling! Nobody is judging you."

"I am going to need a great big cup of hot chocolate with extra marshmallows on top when I finish singing these songs," she said. Christian pulled her into a hug.

"Just think that Vivi is going to be watching you, and she will be so proud of her mother."

"I just hope she gets your singing skills," Meg said, laughing.

A few minutes later, she found herself standing on the platform. Being so short, she was in the very front, of course. And that was the last place she wanted to be. No lip-synching was going to work in this situation.

Christian, being the tallest one there, was all the way on the other end of the platform in the very back. She desperately wished she could slowly slip into the back row.

They started out singing Silent Night, and then the men sang a rendition of Jingle Bells alone. The women followed with O Holy Night. Things were going well, and it surprised her. At least she hadn't fallen off the platform or sang a wrong note.

The last song was finally coming up, and the choir director decided to say a few words. She wasn't sure why the director was stopping the show, as they hadn't practiced that in rehearsal. But at least it would give her a couple of minutes to suck on a cough drop.

"We want to thank everyone for coming out to the Seagrove Christmas festival tonight!" the director, Beatrice, said. The crowd smiled and clapped. "Christmas is the most special time of the year for so many people, and we are thrilled to have something even more special happening tonight. So before we get started with our last song, I'd like to invite one of our members down to the front."

Meg was confused. Now she really didn't have any idea what was going on. Craning her head, she looked down at the twenty-five or so members of the choir, trying to figure out who was being called to the front.

When she realized that Christian was no longer standing in his spot, she was even more confused. She hadn't seen him walk down front. But then there he was, tapping her on the back and taking her hand.

"Christian, what are you doing? I don't want to go over there."

He smiled. "Come with me, my love."

He pulled her out in front of everyone. Never in her life had she wanted to crawl under a set of bleachers so badly.

"What are you doing?" she whispered, a fake smile planted on her face.

"I'm doing something that I should've done long ago." Before she realized what was happening, he started to lower himself onto one knee. It was at that moment that she figured it out.

"Christian..."

He smiled at her. "Meg, you are the most amazing woman I've ever known in my life. Not only are you a wonderful person, but you are an outstanding mother and partner. I can't think of anything else that I would want this Christmas other than to hear you say yes. Will you marry me?"

Her face burned, and she was sure that her cheeks were flaming red at this point. She could feel the adrenaline coursing through every vein in her body, causing her heart to practically beat out of her chest. She covered her face with her hands, trying to will away the tears that were threatening to fall.

"Yes!" she said, jumping up and down. Christian grinned.

His hand shaking, he reached into his jacket pocket and pulled out a small black velvet box. When he opened it, Meg saw the most beautiful ring. It was perfect and everything she would've wanted if she had picked it out herself.

He slid it on her finger before picking her up and swinging her around. The crowd cheered. The director walked over and congratulated them and then told them they didn't have to take part in the last song if they would like to celebrate with family. Thankfully, Christian agreed that was the best course of action and they slipped off into the crowd as their choir mates sang a medley of Christmas songs for the finale.

"Oh my goodness! Congratulations! " Julie said, hugging Meg and Christian.

"Congratulations, man!" Tucker said, shaking his hand.

For the next few minutes, they went down a line of family and friends, giving hugs, high-fives and hand-shakes. When they finally were alone again under one of the large oak trees, Meg looked up at him.

"I had no idea. I can't believe you pulled this off."

He laughed. "Me either. I had to talk you into Christmas caroling just to do this!"

"Wait. You mean that's the only reason you made me do this?"

"Yes, it is. I hope you're not too mad at me."

She chuckled and then hugged him around his waist, pressing her cheek to his chest. "I could never be mad. I was so afraid you would never ask me to get married again."

"And I was so afraid to ask because I thought you would say no."

She pulled back and looked at her ring one more time. "And this is the most beautiful ring I could ever imagine. It looks so custom made."

He held her hand and looked at the ring. "It was my

grandmother's. I had my mother send it to me. She was so excited to hear the news. I just couldn't imagine you wearing any other ring."

Meg hugged him again as Colleen brought Vivi over. She picked up her daughter and realized just how blessed she was. Her family had started in a very unorthodox way, but she wouldn't have changed a thing.

CHAPTER TEN

*A*s Julie helped Janine set up for the cakewalk, she couldn't help but still feel giddy inside about her daughter and Christian getting engaged. As much as she already thought of them as a family, she thought it was wonderful that they would be getting married and making it official. Plus, it would be a great chance to celebrate and have a nice wedding.

"That was one of the most romantic things I've ever seen," Janine said, as she took payment from another person who wanted to take part in the cakewalk. They were raising money for the local homeless shelter just outside of Charleston.

"I know. It was so sweet how he did it. They are lucky to have each other."

Julie continued writing out numbers to put into the hat as Tina walked up.

"I told your daughter congratulations. That proposal was so cute and romantic," she said, smiling.

"Yes, it was. I had no idea he was going to do that.

I'm glad you got to come to the festival. I wasn't sure if you were here."

"Yes, I just got here about a half an hour ago. I wanted to finish up those last few wreaths. I delivered them to the booth."

"Thank you so much for helping with that. I never would've gotten all of that done without your help."

"No problem."

"Make sure that you enjoy all of the different vendors here. I know we've got some wonderful candles down there, and I'm sure there's some great snacks. I think my mom is handing out samples of her poundcake over there too."

Tina rubbed her stomach. "Yes. I've already been by there three times since I got here. I think she's starting to give me the evil eye."

Janine rolled her eyes. "Just ignore her. She can be a bit of a Scrooge."

"I don't blame her. She doesn't know me, and I'm sure she thinks I'm taking advantage of you. Julie, if you and Dawson feel like I've overstayed my welcome..."

Julie held up her hand. "You haven't. We have enjoyed having you there, and you've been so much help to me. She even helped Dylan write his letter to Santa Claus," she said to Janine.

"How long was that letter? He told me the other day what he wanted, and I swear that kid would never stop talking!"

Tina giggled. "I didn't mind. I really enjoyed spending some time with him."

"Well, would you enjoy spending more time with him? Dawson's dragging him around the festival while he helps out, and I'm sure Dylan's bored silly. Do you think you might have some time to take him to visit some different booths here? Maybe get his picture taken with Santa?"

Tina nodded. "I would love that, actually. I'll meet you guys back here when the tree lighting starts."

"Thank you so much. Hey, is that Amy over there?"

Janine and Tina turned around and looked. "Yeah, it looks like it. Maybe we should see if she wants to do the cakewalk?"

Tina turned back quickly. "Well, I'm going to go find Dawson and Dylan. I'll see you guys later." She trotted off before Julie could say anything else.

Amy walked up to the table. "Was that Tina?"

"Yeah. She ran off really quickly. I hope everything is okay. She was going to go help out with Dylan."

Amy looked slightly concerned. "Well, it's good that you're helping her. When is she leaving?"

"We haven't really talked about it, but I think probably the day after Christmas. I mean, she can't exactly stay with us long term."

"Do you think she knows that?"

"I think so. Amy, are you worried about her staying with us for some reason? I mean, she's been really nice to Dylan."

Amy seemed uneasy but shook her head. "No. Not concerned. I just still feel like she looks familiar to me, but I can't place her."

"Well, let's not talk about all that serious stuff right now. Tell me you're going to buy a ticket for the cakewalk?" Janine said, smiling.

* * *

Tina couldn't remember a time when she had so much fun. Walking around with Dylan was putting her in the holiday spirit more than anything else could have. Between the music, the laughter and the enormous amount of Christmas food, she felt like she was in a holiday movie.

"Can I get another one of those peppermint tree bark candies?"

She squeezed his shoulder. "I think you've had quite enough. Your mom is going to kill me for letting you have so much sugar."

"I told Santa all of my Christmas wishes. He said he would keep them in mind, but how in the world is he going to remember all of those things? I don't want him to get my list confused with somebody else's."

"Oh, no?"

"What if some nerdy kid wants a chemistry set? I don't want to accidentally get that. I want the new gaming system, a rock tumbler, one of those all-terrain remote control vehicles..."

Tina laughed. "I know, I know. I helped you write the letter, remember?"

"Oh, right."

"So how do you like living with your new parents?"

Dylan suddenly sat down on a bench, his little legs getting tired. "I like it. I especially like the beach and all the yard. Sometimes, me and Dad go out and throw the football. He's teaching me how to be a fisherman too."

"How does it feel to call him dad?"

"Good. I mean, I had my first dad, and Dawson is my second dad. But I think it's okay to call them both Dad. Do you?"

"I think it's okay to call him whatever you feel comfortable with. He obviously loves you very much."

"Yeah."

"Do you call Miss Julie mom?"

"Yeah. She's the only mom I remember. My first mom didn't want me."

"I bet that's not true. How could anyone not want you?"

"She left me. My first dad told me that. He wouldn't lie to me."

"Your dad told you that your mom abandoned you?"

"I don't know what abandoned means, but he told me she left me behind. She didn't want me anymore."

It pained Tina to hear him say something like that. No child should ever think he was unwanted.

"You know, sometimes adults have their own problems. Sometimes they're sad or they make bad decisions, and they're really sorry."

"Do you think my mom was sorry? For leaving me?"

She nodded. "I'm almost sure of it."

* * *

Julie and Dawson stood next to the Christmas tree, looking around the square for Dylan and Tina. It had been well over an hour since she had last seen them standing beside the ice rink watching other people skate. Dylan wasn't quite ready for ice skates yet.

It wasn't like it was a common occurrence to see ice skating in the lowcountry, anyway. But he had wanted to try it. Thankfully, he became a little too scared once he saw just how thin those blades were.

Julie had felt comfortable allowing Tina to take him around the Christmas festival while she and Dawson were busy. In fact, she had been nothing but kind to Dylan since she arrived. If Julie had ever needed a nanny, Tina might have been one of her choices. But she wasn't busy enough that she didn't have time to raise her son.

"Where are they?" Julie asked, looking up at Dawson. He could certainly see better from his vantage point as a tall man.

"I don't see them anywhere. And you told her to meet us here?"

"Actually, she told me. They're going to be lighting the tree in five minutes, and I don't know where they went. I hope everything is okay."

"Does she have a cell phone?"

"If she does, I don't have the number."

Julie got more and more concerned. What did she really know about this woman? Even though she had trusted her, maybe there was more to the story she didn't know. All kinds of scary scenarios were running through her mind.

"Maybe I'll start walking around and see if I can find them. You wait here," Dawson said. As she watched him walk away, she continued scanning the crowd.

One of her favorite things to watch on TV were those true crime TV shows. Even though they never ended well, she always found them to be very interesting with all the twists and turns. Now, worrying about where Dylan was, she found herself coming up with every scary proposition imaginable.

"They're about to light the tree!" Janine said, giddy with excitement, as she ran over. Janine had always loved Christmas, and even as an adult she got just as excited as she had when they were little.

"Have you seen Dylan? Or Tina?"

"No. Why?"

"I let Tina take him to the booths while we were busy, but she was supposed to meet me here before the tree lighting. Now we can't find her or Dylan, and Dawson has gone to look for them."

"I'm sure it's nothing to worry about. Maybe he's getting his face painted or they ran to get another hot chocolate."

"Yeah. Maybe you're right."

As she stood there, the mayor walked over to get prepared to light the tree. He made some speech that she didn't pay attention to because she was still too busy looking around in the darkness. Suddenly, the mayor hit the switch, lit up the tree, and everybody cheered. But Julie didn't cheer.

She felt her heart rate quicken as it pounded in her chest. Where was her son?

As soon as the tree was lit, Julie made a beeline out of there and started walking up and down the sidewalk looking. She finally ran into Dawson.

"Did you find them?" she asked, her voice shaking.

He shook his head. "I can't find them anywhere."

"Oh, my goodness. What do we really know about this woman? She could've taken off with our child!"

Dawson put his hands on her arms. "Take a deep breath, Julie. I'm sure everything is fine. There's just been some kind of misunderstanding."

"Misunderstanding? Dylan wanted to see the

Christmas tree lighting. He would've never missed this on purpose!"

The two of them started walking and eventually met up with Janine, William, Colleen and Tucker. They all fanned out in different directions before finally meeting in the middle of the square again, and none of them had Dylan.

The tree had been lit ten minutes before, and she had no idea where he was.

"I think we need to speak with the police," Dawson finally said. Hearing him say those words meant that things were serious because Dawson was one of the most levelheaded people she knew.

"Okay, let's get over to the local precinct..."

Just as they all turned around to head toward their cars, Tina and Dylan appeared at the other end of the sidewalk. She was holding his hand, but he looked fine.

Julie's anxiety overcame her as she ran ahead of the group, anger welling within her.

"Where did you take my son? We were about to go to the police!"

Tina looked shellshocked. She stopped, her mouth dropping opening and her eyes widening. "The police?"

"He was supposed to see the tree lighting! Were you trying to kidnap him?" Julie reached out and took Dylan's hand, pulling him close to her.

"She wasn't trying to kidnap me," Dylan said, laughing.

"Then why did he miss the tree lighting? Why didn't you meet us where you said you would?"

"If you would just let me explain," Tina said, holding up her hands. She looked truly apologetic, but Julie couldn't think of a good reason she hadn't met them when and where she said she would. The entire group of them, including Dawson, stood there waiting for an explanation. "I don't mean to be gross, but Dylan had way too many treats today. And he got a pretty terrible stomachache."

"A stomachache?" Julie said.

"I ate a bunch of stuff," Dylan lamented, holding his stomach.

"Anyway, all the shops around here are closed. I thought about trying to find your mother to see if she could let us in to the bakery, but I never did figure out where she went. So we walked down to the gas station so Dylan could use the restroom. It's a pretty long walk…"

"You mean he just had a stomachache and had to go to the bathroom?" Julie said, feeling kind of stupid.

"I'm really sorry that we worried you. I don't have a cell phone so…"

Julie shook her head, hanging it in embarrassment. "I'm so sorry for lashing out at you like that. When you didn't meet us, and then we couldn't find either of you, I just assumed the worst."

"I totally understand. I should have come and told you what was happening, but it seemed like time wasted of the essence. In fact, we barely made it."

"No apologies necessary, Tina. Thank you for taking care of him," Dawson said.

As everybody walked away, Julie was left standing with Tina. Dawson put Dylan on his shoulders and headed back over to show him the Christmas tree.

"I'm so sorry again. I should've given you a chance

to explain, but I was just so terrified that something happened to him."

"I understand. You don't really know me. I mean, we're not really friends or family or anything like that."

"But we are," Julie said. "I think of you as a friend. And I just should've trusted that you wouldn't hurt my child. It's just, I don't really know a whole lot about his past. I don't know if a long lost aunt or cousin could come here to try to take him from us."

"I'm really sorry that I made you worry. I have to get a phone so I can be in communication with people. I would've let you know, but I didn't want him to have an accident."

"You did just the right thing. Thanks for making sure he was taken care of. Do you want to go look at the tree?"

Tina smiled and nodded. "That would be great. I've been looking forward to seeing it."

* * *

Harry stood in the foyer, looking at his daughter. It was time for Carrie to leave, even though it was early on Christmas morning. She had other friends and family to see before the day was over, so she had an early flight to catch. They had done all of their Christmas celebrations on Christmas Eve just so she would have time to catch her flight.

"I can't believe you're already leaving," Harry said, holding her hands.

"Me either. But now that I see where you live and I've met your wife, I feel so much better about leaving you here."

"I'm a big boy, Carrie. I can take care of myself. But I'm going to miss my daughter."

"And I'm going to miss my dad. You better do the video chat now that I've shown you how."

He laughed. "I promise. Video chats every Thursday night. And texts at least three times a week."

"The first person who breaks either of those rules has to buy the other one a fifty-dollar gift card to our favorite coffee shop."

"You have yourself a deal!" Harry said, hugging her tightly. As he backed up, Dixie stepped forward.

"I'm so happy that we finally got to meet, Carrie. I feel like I have a brand new daughter."

Carrie smiled. "I know we started off kind of rocky," she said, quietly. "But I truly believe you're the best thing that has ever happened to my dad, and I know you'll take good care of him."

"I promise you I will." Dixie gave her a long hug. "Did you grab a couple of those fruitcakes?"

"I did! But I will not eat any if I plan to drive because I swear you loaded them down with rum!"

Dixie laughed. "That's the best part of it!"

As they watched Carrie walk out the door and down to her rental car, Dixie couldn't help but feel a little melancholy. Even though Carrie wasn't her daughter by blood, the two of them had become very close while she was visiting, and Dixie hoped that would continue. They had already made plans to fly out to California in a couple of months and spend some time getting to know the area where Carrie lived.

They waved goodbye, and she drove down the road out of sight.

"Well, what would you like to do for Christmas?" Dixie asked as Harry put his arm around her.

"How about we just have a very quiet day here at home?"

She smiled. "How did you know that was exactly what I wanted for Christmas?"

CHAPTER ELEVEN

*I*t was Christmas morning, Julie's favorite day of the year. She was so excited she could hardly wait for Dylan to wake up. The sun was just starting to rise, and she knew as soon as he saw those first glimmers coming through the blinds in his bedroom, he would hightail it downstairs to see what Santa Claus had brought him.

"Good morning," Dawson said, sliding his arms around her as she poured her first cup of coffee.

The house was pretty quiet. Lucy had gone home to see relatives a couple of days before, and Tina hadn't come downstairs yet either.

"Good morning, my handsome husband," she said, running her fingers through the wavy locks of hair around his ears. She loved when he let his hair grow just a bit longer than normal.

"Are you ready to see your present today?"

"Yes! I am more than ready to find out about this

big surprise you've got hiding out in the barn. Shall we go right now?"

"No! Not until Tina and Dylan can go with us. I want them to see just how talented I am!"

She laughed. "I know you're joking, but you are so talented."

"No need to flatter me. I already made your present."

"Care for a cup of coffee?"

"Of course. I'll pour it."

They each got a cup of coffee in the large stoneware mugs she had found at the local thrift shop, and they sat down at the table.

"I bet in about five minutes we're going to hear very excited feet running down the stairs toward the Christmas tree. I can't believe how late we were up last night getting everything ready."

Dawson laughed. "I imagine it's been a long time since you had to stuff Christmas stockings and put out presents from Santa."

"And it was your first time. How did you like it?"

He smiled and nodded. "I could get really used to that."

"You know, as the years go on, the presents get more expensive. And smaller. Before long, you'll look under that tree and think you haven't bought anything, but you'll have spent twice as much!"

"Let's not think about Dylan being a teenager just yet. We have a few good years where our son is still going to want toys and fun things."

As if on cue, they heard Dylan running down the stairs and then squealing with delight when he saw all of his presents lined up under the tree. Tina was right behind him, but obviously trying to stay out of his way.

Like a Tasmanian devil, he ran around the Christmas tree, picking things up, yelling with delight and ripping open every cardboard box. Within a few minutes, it looked like a tornado had gone through the living room, packaging material and tissue paper covering up any of the visible pieces of the floor.

"I guess you like your gifts?" Dawson finally said.

Dylan ran over and hugged him and Julie. "I love them! But I love what Santa gave me most of all!"

That was one of the worst parts of being a parent, Julie thought. Not getting any of the credit for all of those presents that Santa Claus brought.

They sat together, Dawson and Julie drinking coffee while Tina enjoyed an herbal tea. They watched as Dylan enjoyed his first Christmas as a Lancaster. He dumped his stocking on the floor and started munching on candy, with Tina reminding him that stomach aches are not fun.

"I guess I should give Dawson his Christmas present," Julie said, smiling.

Dawson rubbed his hands together. "Oh yeah? Is it a new Ferrari? A trip to Hawaii?"

She tilted her head to the side. "I don't think you've looked at our bank account lately."

"I try not to look," Dawson joked.

A few moments later, she walked over and handed him a box. "I hope you like it."

He opened the box and got very excited. "This is that new toolbox I said I wanted!"

"How that thing was so expensive I will never understand," Julie whispered to Tina.

"Thanks, honey!"

"You're welcome. I expect you to build many more things using that toolbox."

"You know I will!" Dawson said, laughing.

"And, I didn't forget you, Tina," Julie said, walking over to the Christmas tree and picking up a gift bag.

"What? I didn't expect you to get me anything. And I didn't get you anything..."

She handed it to her. "I didn't want you to get me anything. But we wanted to do something nice for you this holiday season."

"You guys have been more than nice to me. In fact, no one has ever done what you have done for me. I couldn't ask for anything more."

"You're not asking. Now, open it."

Julie sat down and waited for her to dig down into the gift bag.

Tina pulled a box out of the bag and opened it to find a beautiful silver charm bracelet. On it, Julie had added three charms. One was a cross for Tina's Christian faith. Another was a starfish to remember her time in Seagrove. The third one was a little Christmas wreath to say thank you for her help at the festival. Julie explained what each charm meant.

"Wow. This is the most beautiful bracelet I've ever seen. Thank you so much!"

Julie stood up and hugged her. "You're very welcome. I hope it will always remind you of the time that you spent here with us. We consider you a lifelong friend, and we expect you to come back and visit sometime."

Tina stood there quietly for a moment, a couple of tears escaping her eyes. "Thank you. Truly."

"Well, ladies, it is now time for the unveiling of the most amazing and wonderful Christmas gift ever given to anyone!" Dawson said, standing up dramatically. He puffed out his chest and held one arm in the air like he was about to give a stirring speech.

Julie playfully hit him in the stomach with the back of her hand. "Did you have to ruin such a beautiful moment with your crazy antics?"

"Actually, I did because I'm about to go nuts to get to show you my gift."

* * *

Dawson took Julie's hand and led her out the back door with Tina and Dylan following. They walked across the lawn toward the big barn where Dylan had first stayed at their house.

"Now, you need to close your eyes when I open the door. All of you," Dawson instructed.

Once they all closed their eyes, Dylan probably peeking, Dawson unlocked the barn and pushed open the two big doors. He had never been so excited to show someone something in his life.

When he was growing up, his father had taught him a lot about carpentry. He'd also been really close to the shop teacher at his high school who showed him many building techniques. He remembered building his first piece of furniture, a little end table for his grandmother, which still sat in the living room.

"Are you ready?" he asked Julie as he helped her step

into the barn without tripping over anything. He caught
Dylan sneaking a peek, but sent him a warning glance.
Dylan quickly closed his eyes again.

"I am more than ready!"

"Okay, open your eyes!"

When Julie opened her eyes, she was staring at the
large walnut dining table that Dawson had made for her.
Long and wide, it would take up most of the dining
room, but it would help to house not only their family
but any guests that were staying at the inn. Plus, they
could use the existing chairs they had until Dawson
could build some custom ones to match.

Not only had he made the table, but he had put a
long section of blue glittery resin down the center
that was covered with polyurethane. It gave the
feeling of the ocean waves right in the middle of the
table. On one corner, he had carved their name,
"Lancaster".

Julie stood there, no words coming out of her mouth
as she stared at the table. At first, he couldn't tell if
maybe she was disappointed and thought she was
getting something else. Then, he noticed tears forming
in her eyes as she walked over and touched the end of
the table with her fingertips. She ran her hand across
the word "Lancaster".

"Dawson, it's the most beautiful table I've ever seen
in my life. How in the world did you come up with this
idea?"

"Actually, I dreamed about it. It's made from walnut,
and I cut the tree down right here on our property. I
had William and Tucker come over and help me one day
while you were at work."

"I love the blue part in the middle," Dylan said, walking over and sliding his hand across it.

"That's supposed to look like the ocean," Dawson said. "The ocean unites us and it's where we became a real family."

"Thank you so much," she said, hugging him tightly. "This table will be in our family for generations."

"I hope so. I worked really hard on this, and I almost ran away from home a couple of times."

Julie laughed. "How are we going to get it into the house?"

"Oh, we will hire some special movers for that!" Dawson said, chuckling. "This thing is heavy as lead, and I have no interest in moving it."

As he watched Julie and Dylan continue to walk around the table and look at it with awe in their eyes, he was proud of all the hard work he put in.

"Why don't we go inside and enjoy breakfast at our current dining table one last time?" Julie said.

"That sounds great. I'm requesting those blueberry pancakes with the little bits of bacon in them you make," he said as he hugged her from behind.

"Oh, you will get anything you want for breakfast after making me that table," she said, laughing.

They all walked out of the barn, Dawson pulling the doors closed behind him. When he looked up, he saw a car pulling into the driveway he didn't recognize.

"Who is that?"

"I'm not sure..." Julie said, squinting her eyes.

It surprised Dawson to see Amy, the head of the foster care system, stepping out of her car. She waved and then called Julie's name.

"I'd better go see what she needs. Why don't you guys go in the house and start setting the table? I'll be in shortly."

* * *

"Merry Christmas! But what are you doing here? Why aren't you with your own family this morning?" Julie asked as she walked toward Amy.

Amy looked upset, almost like she had been given some terrible news.

"I'm sorry to interrupt your Christmas morning."

"Is everything all right? You looked a little rattled."

"Actually, everything isn't all right."

"Why don't we go over here to the picnic table and sit down?" Julie led her over to the old concrete picnic table that had belonged to Dawson's grandmother. She often sat there, wondering about all the conversations that had been had there over the years.

"I don't exactly know how to tell you this."

"You're scaring me..."

"Julie, remember when I saw Tina and kept thinking that she looked familiar?"

"Yeah. You thought you might've known her from somewhere."

"Well, it just kept bothering me, so I ran by the office last night and pulled up Dylan's file."

"Dylan's file? What does that have to do with Tina?"

"There were a few pictures in the file and as soon as I saw this one, I knew exactly who she was," Amy said, pulling a picture out of her purse and sliding it across the table.

"This looks like Tina. I mean, she looks younger..."

"Actually, her name is Christina. I guess she goes by Tina."

"I don't understand."

"Julie, Tina is Dylan's biological mother."

Julie looked up, her eyes widened in shock. "What?"

"I don't know exactly how she found out who had adopted Dylan, but I have to believe this isn't an accident."

"Oh, my gosh. She's inside my house right now, about to have breakfast with my son. She was with him at the Christmas festival the other night. I don't know what she's been saying to him..." Julie jumped up and ran into the house, leaving Amy sitting at the picnic table alone.

She looked in the living room and then ran into the kitchen, ready to confront Tina even though it was Christmas morning.

"What's going on? Are you okay?" Dawson asked when he saw her come into the kitchen so frantically. Thankfully, Dylan was sitting at the table, going through his Christmas stocking again and wasn't paying a lot of attention to his surroundings.

"Where is Tina?" Julie said, seething with a rage she'd never felt before.

"I don't know. I thought she was right behind me but maybe she went down by the beach?"

Julie turned to head back out the door to find Tina.

"Where are you going?"

"To find her."

Even though Amy was calling her name, Julie flew straight past her and ran down the pathway to the beach. Sure enough, she found Tina standing there, at the waters' edge, staring out over the ocean.

"Did you honestly think we wouldn't find out who you really are?" Julie screamed at her.

Tina turned around slowly, a blank look on her face. "I'm sorry for lying to you."

Julie closed the distance between them, but she also realized that she didn't want to get arrested on Christmas day... or any other day... so she stopped herself from lunging and knocking her to the ground.

"Why? Why did you do this?"

"I couldn't help it. I had to know if my son was okay."

"Seriously? Aren't you the same woman who abandoned him when he was a little boy?"

"I see you've been told that story too. And it's not true. "

"Well, it seems pretty true since your son was in foster care and not with his biological mother when we met him."

"Julie, please listen to me. I know you owe me nothing, and I've lied to you for weeks now, but if you'll just let me explain..."

"Were you trying to kidnap him? Is that what was going on at the Christmas festival?"

Tina looked at her, shocked. "What? Of course not! I told you what happened. He had a stomachache."

"Well, excuse me if your words fall flat for me. It isn't exactly like you've been honest with us from the beginning."

Tina took in a breath and then blew it out slowly.

"Look, I didn't come here to interfere. I wasn't going to tell Dylan that I was his mother..."

"I am his mother."

Tina nodded. "In every way that counts, you're his mother. But I wasn't going to tell him that I gave birth to him. I never intended to hurt anyone. I just wanted to see that he was happy, and I can easily see that."

"We invited you here because we thought you were just some random person down on her luck. We didn't want you to spend the holidays alone. And this is how you repay us?"

"Dylan's father was a very abusive man. As far as I know, he wasn't abusive with Dylan, but he was very violent with me. We had only been dating about three months when I got pregnant. He regularly hit me, pushed me down the stairs. One time, I thought I'd lost Dylan. I knew I could never raise him in that environment."

"And yet you left him there."

"In the end, I did. And I regret it every day of my life. I was young and stupid and scared. I had no family really to go to, and I had my own problems. I turned to drugs and alcohol after I gave birth because I couldn't handle living with a violent man."

"How in the world could you choose drugs over your child? And then leave him with a supposed abuser?"

"Look, I know you don't understand because you've never lived through anything like that. But my mind wasn't right at that time. And he threatened me. He told me if I took Dylan with me, he would find us both and he would hurt me. And I didn't have any money. I didn't have a job. I didn't have any way to get an attorney."

"I don't know why you're telling me all of this."

"Because I want you to understand why I never went back for Dylan. I was afraid I wouldn't make it out alive. I had no idea that my ex had gotten into drugs as well. But when I heard through the grapevine that he died, I came looking for my son. And then I learned that he'd been adopted."

"And how did you find us?"

"I guess maybe it's one of the detriments of being a small town. I just did some asking around about foster care opportunities. Before I knew it, I was able to find out about the camp you held, and then someone told me that the people who run the camp adopted one of the kids. It wasn't an accident that I walked into the bookstore that day."

"I can't believe what a liar you are. You really had us fooled. What do you want us to do now?"

"Nothing. I never wanted anything but to see that my son was okay because I have worried about him every day of my life. I don't expect you to ever forgive me or make me a member of your family, but I want you to know that I am going to thank God every day for giving him you and Dawson as parents."

"Have you told Dylan who you are?"

She shook her head. "No. And I don't think we should. It would only confuse him and make him feel pulled between two mothers. He already has the best mother, and I don't want to ever take that away from him."

"So now what?"

"Now, I leave. I spent Christmas with my son," she said, smiling. "There's nothing that could ever top that."

She started walking toward the inn.

"Where are you going?"

"To get my things. I think it's time for me to go."

Julie sighed. "Tina?"

"Yeah?"

Julie had calmed down, although she was still pretty angry. She could feel that Tina's words were coming from a good place, that she had been worried about her son for years, and this had been her only way of checking on him. What would she have done in a similar situation? Would she have lied to get close to her child, even if for just a little while? Probably.

"What are you going to do with your life now?"

"I don't know. But I feel a weight has been lifted from me that has been there for a long time. I'm not sure where I'll go or what I'll do, but I will carry this Christmas with me forever."

"I'd like to give you a little money to get you started in a new life."

Tina stared at her. "Why would you want to do that? After everything I've done?"

Julie walked toward her. "Because my son would want me to do that."

* * *

As Tina pulled away in her little beat-up car, Dawson put his arm around Julie. They stood on the front porch of their home, Dylan happily playing on the floor in the living room behind them.

"I have to say you're very forgiving," Dawson said.

"Oh, forgiveness will take me a while. But I can't

blame her. I might've done the same thing if I were in her circumstances."

"Well, I hope she takes that money and starts a better life for herself."

"Me too."

They turned around and looked through the open front door at Dylan building some kind of superhero play set.

"No matter what happened, I think this has been our best Christmas yet."

Julie looked up at him. "And we have so many more wonderful Christmases to come."

❄

Want to read more by Rachel Hanna? Find many more books on Amazon, Barnes & Noble and Apple!

Join Rachel's private VIP Reader group on Facebook by going to https://www.facebook.com/groups/RachelReaders